Tied Hands in the Fire

A Trilogy of Betrayal

RIKITA SINGLETON

authorHOUSE®

AuthorHouse™
1663 Liberty Drive
Bloomington, IN 47403
www.authorhouse.com
Phone: 1 (800) 839-8640

Published by AuthorHouse 07/06/2017

ISBN: 978-1-5246-9893-5 (sc)
ISBN: 978-1-5246-9892-8 (e)

Library of Congress Control Number: 2017910559

Print information available on the last page.

Any people depicted in stock imagery provided by Thinkstock are models, and such images are being used for illustrative purposes only. Certain stock imagery © Thinkstock.

This book is printed on acid-free paper.

CONTENTS

DEDICATIONS

I would like to dedicate this book to my one and only honey bear Donn Spruill. Honey if it wasn't for you I would not be where I am today. Thank you for being you and pushing me to do things that I am always scared to do. I love you so much.

Red Revenge:

Serena goes her whole life getting hurt time and time again, until she cannot take it anymore. She embarks on a journey to get away and find a new life for herself, but when her past keeps pulling her back in, she has no choice, but to face the same people who hurt her all those years ago.

Kiss of Thorns:

Serena is a woman who always knew what she wanted and trusted who is closest to her. With trust comes deceit. When she meets Charlie he turns her world upside down, but can she trust him to not let her down?

Truth or Lies:

Cassie has always been the kind of person who lies and cheats to get whatever she wants no matter who gets hurt in the process, but when she is put to the test to tell the truth when her sister is kidnapped, will her lies make her loose everything she has ever cared about or will she win the game she is forced to play?

THE RED REVENGE

"It is easy to look at people and make quick judgments about them, their present and their past, but you'd be amazed at the pain and tears a single smile hides. What a person shows to the world is only one tiny facet of the iceberg hidden from sight. And more often then not, it's lined with cracks and scars that go all the way to the foundation of their soul."

— Acheron Dark hunter series

PROLOGUE

"Serena, we have to go now if we are ever going to get out of here."

Serena moaned, but could not speak on account of the pain she was feeling from another beating she had had from her enemy. If she ever got out of this she was going to kill the person who put her in this position in the first place. Serena tried to get words out to lash out at her attacker, but when she opened her eyes, she was shocked. Not only did she not see her attacker she saw the one person who she thought she would never see again, her guardian Savitar.

"I know surprised to see me huh kid. Well since I heard of your little predicament I came straight away, at first I asked nicely then I had to sneak in here to come get you to bring you back. Nobody deserves this."

Savitar cut the chains that held her arms and legs hostage and picked her up and kept her close to his chest and carried her and walked her out of the jail where they had kept her and tortured her for four years.

"We need to get you blood asap kid, you are not looking to good."

"Sa....Sav I......I can't go.......g.....go b...back."

"I know you can't but we don't have a choice. They found out I am getting you back. I will make sure I will protect you. I am your guardian after all. No matter what I will be there. This hallway is too long and I don't want a chance to be seen and get in a fight. So let us take the quick way shall we."

With that they vanished and flashed into the bedroom Serena dreaded seeing again. Savitar carried her and put her gently on the bed Serena spent so many nights crying. Saved from a hell just to be brought back into another one she thought. Savitar bit into his wrist and put it over Serena's mouth.

"Drink up kid, The strongest steel is forged by the fires of hell. Get stronger and maybe just maybe you will leave your own hell once and for all."

Serena drank all that she could. She closed her eyes thinking what her guardian had just told her. She would never get out of this hell she thought. But she made a promise to herself that she would never again be weak, she will become strong, strong enough to end all of the suffering.

CHAPTER 1

Present day

Dreaming of the past again, Serena woke up to another night where she will destroy everyone who had a part in destroying what little life she had back then. She got out of the bed and looked out of the window. It looked so lively and all of the happy tourists of New Orleans didn't even realize the terror that surrounded them at night. They had no worries or cares or even thoughts of vampires or vampire hunters. Tonight Serena couldn't think about that, she had promised her friends one night of fun, while she had the weekend of freedom in her hands. She had a party she couldn't miss. Even if she tried her friend Trista would hunt her down and drag her there herself. Serena put on her black coat while looking at herself in the mirror she looked different, different hair and name, but looking at her wrist where her cuts were she knew she was the same person just different look and name. She put on her sunglasses, and walked out the door.

Serena finally got to her friend Kierien's club. It was crowded for the party tonight, as she went in. When Serena went to sit down at the bar, Trista walked straight over after serving a group of guys their drinks.

"Hey Jude, you decided to come to this party willingly. I don't imagine you are going to dance or sing will you?" Trista said with a smile.

"No, I won't sing, and you know why I don't anymore, but if you need another dancer then I am yours to command."

"Haha, well well, I didn't think that we could get the great big scary Jude to dance. You owe me ten dollars Trist."

Serena looked behind the bar to see Kieren standing there with a big smile on his face.

"Oh so we are betting on me now, I get it I have been MIA lately but I am here right. Does that count for anything?"

"Well, maybe just on your terms, but since we didn't have to come find you, you get some points and you have to dance."

"Fine just say when and I will dance, but I am not changing into any costumes."

"Deal, "Trista said smiling.

Trista gave a beer to Serena while she walked away to take more orders from other customers.

"You know Kierian this is my last night here before I have to go back to New York. You two could be a little sentimental for me."

"Ha, the day you want sentiment from us is the day that I will put on a dress for one week and shave my head bald."

Serena laughed

"I will remember that, that is actually a weird visual. The next time I need something because I am sad I will first come to you and say what dress you are going to wear.

"Ha Ha, very funny. I am going to do my rounds, do you need me before I go?"

"No, I am good, go take care of your customers, I am not staying long anyway. I still need to pack. I am only going to stay for one dance, so tell Trist to make it a good song."

"She only knows the best songs. Later."

Serena sat at the bar when Aimee put a glass of wine in front of her. Serena looked up at Aimee puzzled.

"That man two seats down sent it. I would take the invitation." She said winking and walked away.

Serena looked and she couldn't believe her eyes, she could hardly breathe. All the guy had to do is look at her she thought. That is all he had to do to confirm her suspicions. When he finally looked up those brown eyes that had haunted her dreams time and time again. Same eyes same face same calm cool look as when they first met all those years ago. Quincy walked over to her with the look of recognition on his face.

"Do I know you from somewhere?"

She breathed out slowly, thankful that he didn't recognize her. Her past life was done, she didn't want the past to come back, especially with the man who hurt her.

"No, you don't, you are mistaken."

"Huh, my apologies then, I thought you were someone I knew."

"No worries about it. So if that is it, I would like to get back to being by myself now."

"You know this may seem weird but I found myself drawn to you."

"Well, you shouldn't I am a mess after all. You should go back and find someone new.

"Where are my manners, let me introduce myself. I am Tommy Quincy. People call me Quincy. And you are?"

"Hmm, do you really think you can get my name, I am not that easy."

"Challenged accepted then mystery girl. By the end of the night if I have not gotten your name by any means accident or not I get a kiss and a conversation."

Serena smiled. Quincy was the same as ever, he was the smooth talker he always was. She wished she could get close to him again but it was too dangerous to get close to anyone right now.

"You're on Tommy."

"Quincy, you can call me Quincy."

"Yet Tommy sounds so much better."

"Fine, for you only Tommy it is."

"Don't I just feel all special and warm inside."

"Oh, by the end of the night you will fall in love with me."

"Ha, it is that simple huh."

"Yes, it is."

"Jude, we got a dance number, Our own version of Toxic, do you remember it."

Dammit, Serena thought, Trista always had bad timing.

"Yeah, Trist I remember, but I can't tonight."

"Oh come on, it is a quick version, you know that and it will be fun to have the unholy trinity together again. you, me, Aimee.

"I can't, I have other plans."

Trista left to get to the stage. "I will be right back."

"So, Jude the dancer. That is quite the talent."

8

"You don't even know the half of it. I guess you won the bet huh."

"I think you owe me something" Quincy said whispering in Serena's ear.

Jude felt shivers going down her spine. Jude went up close and up to his ear.

"Later perhaps, I have some business to take care of"

Jude walked off to join Aimee and Trista on stage.

"Quincy we need to go, I found some vampire hunters close to the french quarter."

"I will meet you there Dante, I have one thing to take care of first."

After Jude finished talking to Trista about what was going on she went to the entrance to leave. She had to get back before she had a hunting party after her. She said her goodbyes to Trista and Kieren.

"Be careful Jude, make sure you watch your back, and if you need our help you call us."

"I will Kieren thanks. I will see you in a couple of months or earlier if I am lucky."

Jude was outside about to walk back to her apartment when someone grabbed her arm gently. Serena turned around to find Quincy.

"I am glad I caught you Jude, you weren't just going to leave without saying goodbye were you?"

"Sorry Quincy something urgent came up I got to go."

"Wait, when can I see you again?"

Jude just looked in his eyes, she wanted to walk into his arms and stay there where she always felt safe, but she couldn't not anymore.

"I am not sure."

Quincy took her phone and put his number in it.

"Just in case you get sure sometime, you have my number."

"You are just so sure of yourself aren't you?"

"Haha, I am just confident. I feel like we have known each other forever."

Quincy turned serious while looking at her, he walked up closely to her and kissed her. The past crept up on her the second he kissed her. It felt so familiar. HIs kiss was so fierce and hot yet still tender. She was breathing in the familiar spicy scent of his skin. Oh how she wanted to tell him her real identity, but she didn't have the heart to do it. There was no point of going back to that place in her past especially with how her life was now. One day perhaps, but not again. All too soon he broke the kiss.

"I will see you soon I hope Jude."

Quincy walked away. Jude was happy but at the same time disappointed that he didn't remember her. No reason to dwell on it, it is not like she would ever see him again. But why did the sound of that hurt her so much. Jude looked around and saw no one around. She flashed back to her apartment finished packing and then looked around sadly knowing she was going to miss this apartment while she was gone. She walked back to her motorcycle to go start something that would end her.

CHAPTER 2

Flash Back
Twelve Years Ago

Serena was at a bar with her friend from her dance class Rebbecca. She had snuck away from her parents again. Her parents who had always controlled her fate no matter how much older she got.

"Your parents won't come looking for you will they, I mean for having a vampire for a father and a human for a mother they are the horrific Dynamic Duo, but your rivals the Quincy family I think your family has a run for its money. Why are they fighting anyway?"

"I don't really care, but it is all about control over long island, apparently without humans knowing our two families took control of it. But who the hell cares. They can look all they want they will not do anything in public to reprimand me."

"Well, I have seen you with some bruises, they don't do that to you do they?"

"I said I was just clumsy just leave it alone and let us drink ok."

"Fine fine. I will leave it alone. Just be careful alright. I still like my dancing buddy in one piece."

"And that is how she will be, forever."

The bartender put a martini in front of Serena. Serena looked up at him, and he pointed to the man sitting at the bar. He had messy short brown hair, dark brown eyes, a black t-shirt. A long red coat, blue jeans, and black boots. He almost looked like a bad boy rocker. He looked so laid back, had no worries at all. He also looked powerful and dangerous. For some reason Serena was drawn to this person in more ways than one.

"Looks like you have a fan already. He is cute. You should go say hi."

"Eh, he looks ok, too confident for his own good, and he got my taste of drink so wrong."

"Ah come on he has to gain some points for effort. I am going to waive him over here."

"No don't…"

But it was too late the stranger was already walking over while Rebbecca got up to leave.

Quincy had finally found his prey. The enemy to his family, he was sent to kill as a warning that Long Island was theirs and theirs alone. First looking at her, her short dark brown hair was laced with auburn strands that caught the light. Her dark brown eyes showed her intelligence yet innocence. Every day that he followed her when she danced she had such grace, and danced beautifully. The need rose in him to taste those parted lips as he saw her talking to her friend Rebbecca. He shut that down quickly she was just another mark his family sent to kill, the only thing he was ever good at or worth to his family. He sent her a drink, he only had to get her alone long enough to finish the job. When the drink got sent it didn't look like she was happy to be receiving a drink by him which is unusual because usually woman are drawn to him, until her friend waived him over to their table. So let the hunt begin he thought.

Serena tried to get up and walk off after Rebbecca who had left her alone to confront the stranger but it was too late he had already come and sat across from her. If she left now it would be rude to leave. After getting a closer look at him, he truly did have a dangerous appearance. His face looked so cold and calculating, but when he got to the table and looked at her, he noticed the only person he actually smiled for was her. She had to admit to herself even with his dangerous appearance he was sure sexy.

"Where did your friend go?"

His voice was mesmerizing, his voice was so deep it reminded her of thunder.

"Well, apparently she left so we can have alone time, which I didn't want."

"I am not that bad am I?"

"Sorry, it is not you, I don't talk to strangers much. Call it a habit."

"Well, for you my dear I won't be a stranger for long."

"Oh really, Mr. Cocky, what makes you say that"

"Well, at the end of the night you are going to fall in love with me."

"Just like that?"

Just like that."

"You don't even know my name."

"I am confident that I will earn it."

"Does that work with all the girls you meet. You buy them a drink and they just give in to your confidence."

"Ha ha usually."

"Well, wrong girl to try it on."

"Ok, if I can guess your name will you give me a chance."

"You get only one try."

"Serena"

Serena stopped smiling and stared at him cautiously.

"How did you know that?"

"I heard your friend say it when I was coming over."

"Damn, I hate that you have good hearing."

"I guess you owe me a chance huh?"

"Fine I owe you that much. So you know my name what is yours?"

"My name is Tommy Quincy"

"Quincy it is."

"You realize my first name is Tommy right or Tom for short."

"Quincy sounds so much better though right?"

"Haha, do you always do the opposite of what someone expects."

"It is the only way I know how to live."

They both laughed.

"Ok, only for you, you get to call me Quincy."

"Aren't I just special."

"Are you always this witty?"

"I was born having a witty mouth."

"Ha ha, I like that you are witty, it is different, a lot of girls don't have that."

Rebbecca came back and ran up to Serena.

"Serena….."

Rebbecca paused as she saw the guy from the bar.

"What is it Becca?"

"You have a situation, they are here."

"Who is here?"

Rebbecca pointed toward the entrance and two guards from her parents house were there. When they saw her they walked straight to her.

"How did they find me?"

"I don't know, but we have to go now."

"What is going on?"

Serena turned and looked at Quincy, he was cute, but she couldn't socialize with anyone, if anything the guards coming brought her back to reality.

"Don't worry about it, I need to go. It was nice meeting you."

"Hey girl, we are here to take you home. Come with us now."

"I have a name you know, and tell those people I am out, you never saw me ok."

"Looks like we have to force you since you are being disobedient. Which is what I was hoping you would do."

The guard punched her so hard across her face, she fell into the empty table next to the table she was sitting at. She sat up wiping the blood on her lip. Since her parents owned this club everyone just stayed where they were and went ahead with business as usual. No one ever butted in with my parents business, they minded their own so they wouldn't feel the wrath of the people who owned Long Island, well half of it anyway. Serena got up slowly with her cheek swollen red with a bloodied lip.

"Is that all you got, because even my dance teacher tortures me better than that."

"Hey guys, wasn't Serena already being resistant, the king said to bring her however means necessary." The rest of the guards laughed.

"Let her go. She didn't even do anything to you, I will take her home." Rebbecca said trying to get to Serena but was blocked off by the rest of the guards.

"Becca just stay out of it would you. I will be fine. Go home ok please, I will see you tomorrow."

Rebbecca was about to say something further but looked at the pleading look in her friend's eyes, she knew if she tried to stop it now they both would be in trouble.

"Fine, I will see you tomorrow." Rebbecca said before walking out the door.

"Now where were we before we got rudely interrupted. Oh yeah, we were trying to forcibly get you home." The guard said smiling.

The guard punched Serena in the stomach and she crouched down to the ground while holding her stomach. He was about to punch her again when a hand stopped him.

CHAPTER 3

She is very interesting Quincy thought. No woman had ever been able to resist him before human or vampire. But this halfling could. She wasn't classically beautiful, but there was an exotic quality to her dark brown eyes that gave her charm. Her short brown hair was loose, spilling past her shoulders. Her eyes were captivating showing her intelligence and warmth and innocence. They met his eyes equally, like he was just another person who would soon be against her. Right now they were narrowed at him with curiosity. She was the prettiest curious woman he had ever seen and all he wanted was to take her into his arms and kiss her, make her lips swollen from his kisses. He had to get that thought out of his head. No matter what he had wanted to do, he knew that she was the target, he could never get attached. He was going to ask if she wanted to take a walk outside so he could finish what he had started when her friend came back. He was almost there he thought.

"What is going on?"

Quincy asked baffled. Did they know who I was, did they figure out my family's plans to kill their daughter.

"Don't worry about it, I need to go. It was nice meeting you."

"Hey girl, we are here to take you home. Come with us now."

"I have a name you know, and tell those people I am out, you never saw me ok."

"Looks like we have to force you since you are being disobedient. Which is what I was hoping you would do."

The next thing Quincy knew the guard had punched her so hard across her face, she fell into the empty table next to the table she was sitting at. She sat up wiping the blood on her lip. Since her parents owned this club everyone just stayed where they were and went ahead with business as usual. No one ever butted in with my parents business either, they minded their own so they wouldn't feel the wrath of the people who owned Long Island, well half of it anyway. Serena got up slowly with her cheek swollen red with a bloodied lip.

"Is that all you got, because even my dance teacher tortures me better than that."

Quincy had to admit that she was brave, she faced them head on with that wit of hers narrowing her eyes with malice. How could her parents knowingly know that the guards treat her like this he thought.

"Hey guys, wasn't Serena already being resistant, the king said to bring her however means necessary." The rest of the guards laughed.

"Let her go. She didn't even do anything to you, I will take her home." Rebbecca said trying to get to Serena but was blocked off by the rest of the guards.

"Becca just stay out of it would you. I will be fine. Go home ok please, I will see you tomorrow."

Quincy was looking into the background, this innocent woman was getting beaten on and she told her only friend to go home. She probably knew her friend would get it too. Shame, someone had to stick up for the girl.

"Fine, I will see you tomorrow." Rebbecca said before walking out the door.

"Now where were we before we got rudely interrupted. Oh yeah, we were trying to forcibly get you home." The guard said smiling.

Quincy was about to walk out of the bar, when he heard what the guard had said. He had thought they were going to take her home after that. They were going to humiliate her even more. Isn't she supposed to be the first girl in the vampire society one day. He had one hand on the door knob. Screw it he thought. He was the only one who could stand up to them, he could destroy her later. Quincy just caught the guards hand as he was going to deal the final blow.

"Who the hell are you?" The guard said narrowing his eyes.

"It doesn't matter who the hell I am, touch that girl again and you are a dead man."

The guard laughed as he snatched his arm back from Quincy's grasp.

"Do you know who the hell I am. I am the Harrison's best guard. But I almost hate to kill you, out of all the people I have bested in fighting, you have one good sense of humor."

"Well, I aim to please." Quincy put himself between Serena and the guards. "Now why don't you call it a night and just leave this girl alone, huh."

"How about no."

Quincy grabbed her hand so she wouldn't get hurt by the fight.

Serena was in awe by this man she hardly knew. He was either crazy or borderline insane. She knew one thing he knew how to fight. He clipped the first guard with his elbow, then sent him flying head over heals on to the bar floor. He caught a second guard by the throat and slammed him into the floor and knocked him out with one single punch. A third came running. Acting on instinct, Serena whirled around and kicked him back with her leg. She caught him in the groin and he went down to the floor whimpering.

Quincy arched his eyebrows in surprise.

"Don't ask."

"Fine, we need to get you out of here now."

Quincy took her hand and teleported her to his apartment. When they were there he went to the bathroom to get a cloth. When he came back Serena was sitting at the kitchen table.

"I got a cloth for you. Put it on your lip."

"Where are we?"

"My place, sorry I couldn't think of anywhere to take you princess."

"Don't call me that. I hate that word."

"What, princess, isn't that what you are."

"I am just a normal woman, I don't need to be treated special just because of the family I was born into. So if you will excuse me."

"Wait, sit down, I am going to make sure you are ok and then you can go."

"Why did you help me, do you have a death threat or something?"

"Haha, well if I knew I was going to get a thank you like this then maybe I do."

Serena looked away with a slight blush on her face. She was embarrassed.

"Thank you for saving me, but you didn't have to."

"Well, maybe I didn't do it for you, maybe I just like fighting." Quincy said with a smile.

"You are one crazy vampire."

He laughed hard at that. "I am glad I can entertain."

Serena sat back down and put the cloth on her lip.

"Did you want any food or anything before I take you home."

"I am good thank you."

Ok, I have two bathrooms, one is past the first one and the second door next to the bedroom. I am going to take a quick shower and then I will take you."

"You have done enough on my behalf I can just transport home."

"It is fine, plus the beating you just took I am sure you are not strong enough to do it yet."

Serena looked away shyly. He was right she thought. As a halfling she wasn't as strong as normal vampires were.

Quincy had to smile as she blushed. She looked so cute, it made her eyes a full shades darker. He wondered what she would look like after a full night of raw sex. He could see her dark eyes full of passion, her hair mussed, and her cheeks red from his whiskers. The thought made his entire body burn.

"I will be back."

CHAPTER 4

Quincy let the water slide over his body. His shoulder throbbed from when the guy hit it. The only thing that held his attention was the woman who was in his kitchen. Why was he so attracted to her. He had claimed many women over the years and have targeted a lot of people. He had felt nothing for them other than a passing curiosity. And yet this woman tugged at his heart he thought he had gotten rid of a long time ago. It was forbidden for him to fall for a target especially an enemy of his own family. He was born to kill and be forever alone in this world. Never before had that bothered him.

"Oh, come on Quincy," He said as he bathed himself. "Get her the hell out of this house, kill her and go home. Forget you ever saw her." Pain cut through him at the thought of never seeing her again. Still he knew what he had to do. This was his life and he was bound by oath to his family no matter what he felt toward them. He would be leaving soon after this one last job to go be apart of the vampire society in New Orleans. His duties were his family. His loyal oath is his heart. His job was his love, and it would be that way for eternity.

After walking around the apartment and watching a little tv while Quincy was busy, Serena went to go to the bathroom to go put the cloth back and wash her face a bit. She passed the bathroom at the same time Quincy was coming out of the first one wrapping a towel around his waist. They slammed into each other. Quincy put his hands on her shoulders as he finally recognized her. Serena froze as she realized her bracelet was caught in the loop of the cloth. Her heart beat faster at the sight of all that lean power and strength. At the smell of his clean warm skin. His hair was slicked back from his face. She doubted any man could compare to how handsome he was. He fixed those dark eyes on her. The raw hunger in them made her quivery and hot. He looked like he could devour her. And in truth she wanted him too.

"Isn't this quite interesting." Quincy said with a hint of amusement in his voice.

Serena didn't know what to do while her hand was so close to the bulge underneath the towel. Why was it that she was so attracted to him. Her gaze slid over the scars covering his body. She wondered what he possibly could have done to get those scars.

"Trust me you never want to know." Quincy whispered as he moved his hand to cup her cheek.

"What?" She asked realizing he was answering her thoughts.

"You never want to know where I got these."

"How did you know what I was thinking?"

"Haha, because you thought out loud. Next time if you want your thoughts to be private don't ask or say anything out loud.

Serena wasn't really paying any attention. His body was well toned. Her face was so flamed up, she had to look away. Slowly he tilted her chin so she was looking up into her eyes. Before she could move he kissed her. He left her lips and trailed kisses to her throat and back to her lips. She surrendered to him and put her arms around his bare shoulders. He whispered, "You are very tempting princess, but I need to take you home. He took the towel from her bracelet and then went into the bedroom to get dressed. Suddenly she remembered why she came back here in the first place and went into the second bathroom to wash her face.

Quincy leaned against the door with a raging need inside him to pull her back to him. He had to put her out of his thoughts. She was a target, he was supposed to be killing her not kissing her. "I am such a fool," he snarled as he went to dress. He opened the door and found Serena standing in the kitchen waiting for him.

"Are you ready to go?"

"Yeah."

"Ok, I am taking my car, since I don't know where you live we can't transport there."

"Ok."

As they finally got to Serena's house she thanked him one last time and went into the house. Quincy wanted to call her back but he knew he couldn't if she only knew what he had planned for her she would have never kissed him like that. He drove off.

Serena went into the house wishing that Quincy had called her back, but she knew they could never be together. If he only knew what her family was really like he would never want to be with her. But it was still nice to have a person who cared for her at least for a little while. Serena walked in the front doors, the guards probably came back and told my parents what happened by now. She went in and stood tall as she went straight to her parents room.

"Where the hell have you been?! Serena's father went up to her and slapped her across the face.

"Well, Klaus, I was enjoying my night off away from you."

Klaus slapped her again.

"Klaus, stop, you know we need her, she is the face of our family, next to me."

"I am sorry my darling, it is hard to remember when you have a daughter who is dim witted." Serena's mother Haley was sitting up in the bed looking more smug than ever. Serena never liked her parents, she always wanted to escape from them, but she never had the chance, one day she would be rid of them for good.

"Get out of my sight you stupid girl. You don't think we know what you have been doing, we have people follow you everywhere, You are not allowed to dance in anything other than what we choose for you. Or allowed to play any other instrument other than piano. We also threw out most of the clothes you had in your closet. You will dress like a lady. Do you understand. You are the face of this family."

"You mean the face of crooks and liars you mean. You and our apparent enemies who are trying to take control of Long Island New York." Serena's father slapped her again.

"Be quiet you ungrateful brat, just get out of my sight before I trap you in the basement."

Serena narrowed her eyes, but didn't say anything, she walked out quietly not wanting to go into the basement again. Alone in the dark with no food or light at all. When she walked out she saw a man leaning against the wall in the hallway. Her guardian always knew when she was back in the house. He was always there for her no matter what. The only person whoever remotely she considered as her real father. He had short messy silver hair, with golden colored eyes he had a muscular laid back feel, with two silver earrings. But she knew he could be lethal when he had to be. He is the one who taught her how to do the kick she had done tonight. With everyone he always looked stoic, but with her he is the only one who he smiled and talked gently, and joked around with. He was wearing his usual look of a white unbuttoned shirt, with black jeans and black boots, his sunglasses were placed on top of his head.

"Hey kid, how was the night out?" he said with a smile on his face.

"I think you already heard about that, sir." Serena said while walking to her room. Savitar walked to catch up to her.

"You know what I did hear, that you kicked someone's ass. All three actually."

"I only kicked one guy, and surprisingly it was in that sensitive place that hurts him the most which made me extremely happy."

Savitar laughed. "It looks like what I taught you is actually helping."

"Eh, you are ok."

"I also heard you were all cozy with some guy, who attacked the guards on your behalf."

"He is no one, don't worry about him."

"I am not, but if you ever come home unhappy I know what he looks like."

"I am not planning on seeing him again anyway." Serena said as they finally got to her room."

"Why is that?"

"Sav, look at my family, you know why."

"Well, I don't know about you but you could use a little fun. I have a plan."

"What do you mean?"

"I will be your out. Every weekend a month, I will cover for you while you go do whatever fun thing finds your fancy. Ok kid."

"Why would you do that for me, what is in it for you?"

"Well, your happiness, and all that stuff. Whatever. Do we have a deal or not kid. You know I will always be there for you."

"You are worse with feelings than I am. Thank you. We do have a deal." Serena smiled her voice with a little amusement.

"It starts tomorrow, enjoy." Savitar said while walking down the hallway.

"What to do while not looking over my shoulder every few seconds. Only one thing to do." Serena said while walking into her room.

CHAPTER 5

Serena left the house the next night to stay at Savitar's apartment for the weekend. She took Savitar's black Lamborghini to her favorite place in all of Long Island. As Savitar promised as far as she could tell no one was following her. She drove until she got to the music shop she went to every weekend. No one was ever around on the weekend. She was here so much the owner gave her the key so she could play the piano and sing. When she went in she moved her hand down the keys as she sat down taking in the beautiful baby grand piano. It was a beautiful sight. She gently put her fingers on the keys and started playing and singing Let Me Fall.

Quincy woke up the next evening sure that he was going to get his target this time. He followed her from her house at a close distance on his motorcycle so he wouldn't be seen. He had to admit she was good at making sure she wasn't followed. He noticed that she finally stopped at this music shop. Here was his chance. This place is secluded enough with no one else around tonight. He took his bow and arrow and went around the building to see if she was around any windows. He finally found her and set up to take that shot to end her. He had it all ready and pointed it right at her through the window while she wasn't looking. He paused for a few seconds listening to her. She was an angel singing like that. A little musical angel. He couldn't help but smile when he saw her. She was so beautiful, it felt like there was nothing else in the world except the two of them. "I can't do it." He said while slowly putting the arrow down. He knew that she was more than just a target to him. I am more than just curious. He wanted to get to know this woman who had found her way into his lonely heart. He wanted her like no other man would. He packed up his equipment and put it in his car. Then he walked over to see her.

Serena finally finished playing the song when she heard a slow clap from the entrance of the room. She looked up from the piano startled, and saw Quincy staring at her.

"I am sorry I startled you, I heard music from in here and saw an angel singing."

Serena laughed. "Does that line always work for you?"

"Haha, I have only used it on you so you tell me."

"Eh, it could use some work."

They both laughed. Quincy went to sit next to Serena on the piano bench.

"So Quincy what are you doing here?"

"I was out for a walk. Just to get away from everything."

"No really are you following me or something, no one hardly knows this place at all."

"I was just out for a walk that is all. Anyway, you are really good. Where did you learn to sing like that and play like that?"

Serena blushed hearing that, not a lot of people had ever heard her sing and play. Only two people have ever seen it.

"Umm…Well, don't you dare tell anyone. You are only the third person to ever hear. Not a lot of people will like the fact that I do this this well. I learned from my friend Rebbecca."

"I feel honored that I heard it. It will be our little secret hm. Anyway, is that why you are here all alone?"

"Eh, I have a whole weekend to be by myself, I just need to get away from my life as a princess you know."

"It can't be that bad, you are a princess after all."

"HA, more like a prisoner in my own home. You saw how those guards treated me, my father ordered that to be done. And my mother, talk about spoiled. She even….."

"Even what?"

"Nothing, Lets save that for another day shall we."

"I wanted to ask you the other night about this but."

"What?"

What happened to your wrist. When I took the towel I saw the cut."

"Noticed that did you?"

"Is it personal?" Serena looked down touching it, then looked at his eyes, she was ready to tell someone.

"I was a kid, I was eight years old when this happened. My father had just beaten me for being out so late with Rebbecca. He doesn't allow me to have friends. Anyway I went into the bathroom crying like always, wondering what I did to my parents to deserve this. I look over and saw a pair of scissors and decided enough was enough. I was dying slowly when one of my parents guards found me and took me to his place, and brought me back to health. He said that he didn't want to see that again. He had always been keeping an eye on me watching me. He said he was going to be my guardian, made sure he would protect me no matter what. I look back on that day and I regret, but it would have taken away all of that pain I felt." Serena looked up into Quincy's eyes.

"I am sorry, I can't believe your parents would ever do that to you at all."

"It is nothing, I would like to stop talking about it if you don't mind."

"I will Change the subject. Do you have any other talents?"

"I dance a little, some contemporary. My parents wanted me to dance ballet but I expanded to different styles. No one has ever seen them though."

"Can I see?"

"Oh no, I haven't perfected the dances yet and despite my witty tongue that you have heard I am actually shy."

"It will be our secret promise."

Serena sighed heavily. "Fine, ok, but don't laugh."

"Lips are sealed." He mimicked zipping his lips and locking them with a key.

Serena went to her phone and turned on Nocturne in C Sharp Minor by Dejan Lazic, she walked in the middle of the floor and started dancing. When she finally finished, she was breathing hard and blushing. She went up to Quincy and waited for the bad comments to come. Quincy stood up smiling.

"It was so bad you are going to leave right? I know, I don't know why I did that dance in the first place......."

She couldn't get the rest of the sentence out. He pulled her into him and kissed her passionately on the lips. Serena felt like her whole body was on fire from just that one kiss. When he finally pulled away he was breathing heavily.

"Serena, that was beautiful. I could feel every emotion you had in your dance. You were hypnotizing, I never wanted to take my eyes off of you. In that one moment I think you just took my breath away."

Serena blushed and looked away, but Quincy turned her face back. He brushed a strand of hair behind her ear.

"Quincy we can't do this. I can't allow you to come into my world it is too dangerous."

"Danger ha, I laugh at danger. Plus if it is so dangerous I could be your protector couldn't I?

"I don't need a protector."

"Maybe not, but you keep getting into trouble like last night, I would have to show those guys why exactly they shouldn't mess with you."

"Hahaha, why shouldn't they hmm?"

"Because my dear little graceful goddess, you are now mine, and I take care of what's mine."

"I am yours? How are you so sure of this?"

"I knew the moment I first saw you. That I was drawn to you." Serena was speechless as she couldn't look away.

"I see so much pain in your eyes, I want to take away that pain for you." Before Serena could stop herself, she stood on her tiptoes and captured his lips with her own. He moaned at the contact and cupped her face in his hands while he returned the kiss. Push her away he thought, but he couldn't, not tonight. They both needed to feel love again. He could tell in her eyes that she has had a tough life. Right or not he wanted to know the softness of a woman's hands on his body. Serena's scent on her skin. He lifted his head up for only a moment and stared in her dark brown eyes that hunger for him.

"Are you sure that you want to do this Serena?"

"I am sure. I want you Quincy, I have since the first time we kissed." He looked in her eyes and found no doubt. He kissed her again more passionately.

CHAPTER 6

Two years later

Serena couldn't wait to see Quincy this weekend. They have been seeing each other for two years. He was her safe haven away from her parents from everything bad in her life. Lately he had been acting distant, she has asked countless times what was wrong with him but he just said never to worry about it. She would trust him, but deep down inside she knew something was wrong, and until he told her what it was, she was not going to badger him about it until he was ready to tell her.

Quincy walked into his parents home, he knew this was coming sooner or later. The day his parents would send his brother after him to give them an update on killing Serena. He was surprised that he was able to sneak around this long being with her. No matter what happened he wouldn't let them hurt her.

"Dear brother, you are in trouble. You have not been able to deliver the news that the dear daughter of Klaus is dead."

Ignoring him, He walked past his brother until he was in front of his parents in their study room.

"Quincy, how nice of you to finally come to us."

"Before you get started I would like to say one thing. I am done with this. I am not going to kill that innocent girl I am done killing."

"Oh really what about your oath and your family?"

"Screw oath, I have been killing for you since I could remember, I will not do this for you. Especially to an innocent person."

"She is not innocent, she is our enemy. If you do not do this then you leave this family and never come back."

"Well, Father, Mother, and Brother, it was nice knowing you. If any of you follow me I will know. I will make sure I won't tell any one of your crimes. Good bye."

After Quincy left his brother Elijah walked up to his parents.

"Father, what did you want to do about that situation. It is apparent since I found out that Quincy has been dating her, she has been clouding his judgment."

"I have a plan to satisfy my family and the Harrison's my dear boy, she will die, but in due time. I just have to make a quick call. Elijah, Catherine leave me."

After they left, he made a quick call.

"Hello."

"Klaus, long time no talk my friend."

"Nick, what the hell do you want."

"I thought you would be interested to know my son and your daughter have been dating each other it would seem."

"She would never do that."

"I have proof if you want to look at it."

"No need, she has been a thorn in my side ever since she was born. Why are you calling me about it?"

"Do you even care what happens to your daughter, I am just curious father to father."

"Do I care no, but she is the face of our family, but I could care less about her. Why do you ask?"

"I have a deal to make with you. I don't like my son dating your daughter. Now, we can try everything we can to stop them or get rid of one of them and send a message to them saying not to mess with an enemy."

"Are you really suggesting that we destroy one to send a message to the other."

"Exactly. My son is too good to break, you know that you have met him. The one person we could break is your girl. What do you say? And before you say no, let's just say, that the two of us will finally have an understanding. I will leave Long Island to you. If I get a percentage of every single deal you work on. Do we have a deal Klaus?"

"Deal, how do we do this?"

"Leave that to me."

"Hey kid, knock knock, this letter came for you. You are just lucky I got it before your parents guards could lay a hand on it.

Serena looked up from her book to find Savitar in the door way holding an envelope.

"Who is it from that I need to hide it from dear old Klaus and Haley?"

"Well, your guy for one."

Serena ran up to Savitar but he held the envelope from her reach.

"Hey, what is up with you give me the letter."

"When am I going to meet this guy of yours?"

"Haven't you already met him? As my guardian I know you have already seen him before."

"Haha, not up close and personal. That kind of thing."

"If I promise soon do I get the letter?"

"I guess, but I am happy that he makes you happy. That is all I want." He finally gave her the letter.

"Thanks Sav." She opened the envelope and read it carefully.

"He wants to meet, do you think you can cover for me while I go?"

"Of course I can, where are you going?"

"My secret place."

"The music shop you go to. Got it." Savitar said with a hint of amusement in his voice. "Get going kid, I will make sure I won't wait up."

Serena left to go get ready, and went to the music shop.

When Serena parked and went inside she couldn't find Quincy at all. Maybe he was late she thought.

"AH!!!!!" Serena went down on the ground, in pain. She looked down and someone had shot an arrow in her thigh. She was breathing heavily. She looked around until she found a man walking toward the window that the arrow had flown through. She tried to get up and walk toward the door, but the arrow was in too deep she just went back down. She tried to crawl she was almost to the door when the man dragged her back into the room by her leg.

"Oh no no no, my dear Serena, why would you want to leave, that is so rude." The man said while smiling evilly.

"Who the he…..Hell are you?"

"Well, you can call me your maker. But everyone knows me as Elijah. Isn't that right daddy?" Serena saw a man walking toward Elijah, she knew it was Nick. She could never forget a face like that.

"Nick, to who or what do I owe the displeasure of your company?"

"Well, my dear Serena," AH!!!!! Serena yelled as he pushed the arrow further in her thigh. You are talking to a man that happens to be a son of mine."

Serena laughed. "I didn't know evil could have children. AH!!!! YOU only have one son anyway, Him!!!. I never even talked to him let alone met that bastard."

"Oh, you didn't know, I have another son. One you have gotten quite cozy with. And his name is Tommy Quincy I believe. Better yet known as Quincy."

"N...No, why didn't he tell me?"

"Well, there was that thing where I sent him to kill you. You were just his target sorry. Well, actually not too sorry." He said while laughing.

Serena didn't know what to say, she didn't want to believe it was true, but Quincy had said that he had always wanted to tell her something but to afraid to tell her the truth. No, she wouldn't believe it she thought. She would learn the truth from Quincy no matter what. All of a sudden she felt pain in her stomach. Elijah had kicked her in the stomach.

Serena coughed. "Is that all you got, my father hits harder than that."

"If that is the case, let us introduce another guest shall we. A person who helped orchestrate this whole plan." Nick said. "Behind door number one is…"

Serena looked up to see her own father. Klaus, I know yo...you hate me but why?!"

"Aw my dear Serena, you are such a liability. You make bad choices. You will never understand what it means to be in this family. I gave you so many chances, and you failed each time. Nick, are deal still stands, I give her to you to do what you will and you give me Long Island."

"Are deal still stands."

"I hope to never have to see you again. Good bye Serena." Serena just looked shocked that her own father would just walk away from her. "YOU COWARDLY BASTARD." She called after him while he walked out without a care in the world.

"So dad, what are we going to do with her?"

"Well, not kill her yet, but torture, first then death if she begs for it."

"Why the hell are you doing this to me. AHHHHHH!!!!" Nick pulled the arrow out of her thigh and slapped her.

"First I wanted to send a message to your father so I can gain Long Island. But then my son found out something interesting. Well, saw something. He saw a kiss in a bar between the two of you, and that just did not do so well with me, especially since I sent him to kill you. So I am doing what he obviously can't. By sending him a message that he is not allowed to disobey me. Elijah grab her and lets take her back home to our basement. You are not going to see light for a very long time Serena. You will get no food or blood, and you will never again see anyone you remotely call a friend ever again. You are mine now."

"Do your worst you coward."

"Oh I plan to."

Quincy had left his apartment to meet Serena at the music shop. They were supposed to meet tonight. Tonight he would tell her everything. When he walked in he stopped. Something was different, he couldn't place it, but he knew something was different. He called out for her but there was no answer. He went into her favorite room. He stopped when he stepped into something wet. He looked down and saw a pool of blood and noticed a note. He picked it up and saw three words. "She is Mine." He didn't know where she had gone or who took her, but he knew he should have told her who he was in the first place. The enemies he had. He was going to look for her no matter how long it took.

CHAPTER 7

Two years later

"Someone is here for you Serena. Are you ready for your torture today." Serena couldn't say anything but moan as she heard Elijah's voice. They had tortured her to the brink of death. They had even taken advantage of her. Different people different day. Still she wouldn't beg for mercy or beg for death. She was stronger than this. Soon she would get away she knew she would. One way or another.

"D....Do...you....your are worst."

Savitar was getting impatient. He looked everywhere, even followed Quincy and he still turned up with nothing on Serena's whereabouts. Every time he went to Klaus and Haley about it, they just said she was taking a vacation she so rightly deserved. He would never believe that, they never let her out of their sight for a few minutes. He was going to find her, and bring her back, he just hoped he brought her back alive. There is only one person that he could go to that knew everything that went on. He transported to Damien's room. He knew Damien's schedule, he should be coming in a little bit he thought. He sat at Damien's desk. He heard a key enter the lock and the door open.

Damien Jumped as he saw Savitar at his desk.

"Savitar you scared me. What the hell are you doing here?"

"You know why I am here."

"Nope, not a clue."

"Damien, I am being calm right now for a reason. You play both sides. My side and Klaus's side. One reason I am being calm is I like you, I don't want to hurt you. So tell me what I want to know or you better believe I will put my hand through your chest and take out your heart and make you watch while I destroy it." Savitar said wth a calm smile on his face.

"I don't….."

"WHERE IS SHE!!!!!!"

"She is with the Quincy's. Klaus made a deal with Nick in order to gain control of Long Island and Nick gets a percentage of each deal they make so he still is a little in charge. He also wanted to teach his son Tommy a lesson for being with her apparently."

"That is why he was so busy lately. Where did he take her?"

"She is at Nick's house. I am sorry, you know I can't tell you." But she is still alive. They broke her pretty badly Sav."

"It is fine, I know they have something on you. I will deal with that when the time comes. I know we have our arrangements of you giving me information. The only person you actually talk to is Serena. I will find out why someday." Savitar got up and went to the door.

"She saved me that is why I tell her straight, but I still betray her, yet she understands why. What are you going to do?"

"I am going to get her and bring her back. I have a feeling that that family won't be around for much longer."

"Serena, we have to go now if we are ever going to get out of here."

Serena moaned, but could not speak on account of the pain she was feeling for another beating she had had from her enemy. If she ever got out of this she was going to kill the person who put her in this position in the first place. Serena tried to get words out to lash out at attacker, but when she opened her eyes, she was shocked. Not only did she not see her attacker she saw the one person who she thought she would never see again. Her guardian Savitar.

"I know surprised to see me huh kid. Well, since I heard of your little predicament I came straight away, at first I asked nicely then I had to sneak in here to come get you to bring you back. Nobody deserves this.

Savitar cut the chains that held her arms and legs hostage and picked her up and kept her close to his chest and carried her and walked her out of the jail where they had kept her and tortured her for four years.

"We need to get you blood asap kid, you are not looking to good."

"Sa....Sav I......I can't go.......g.....go b...back."

"I know you can't but we don't have a choice. They found out I am getting you back. I will make sure I will protect you. I am your guardian after all. No matter what I will be there. This hallway is too long and I don't want a chance to be seen and get in a fight. So let us take the quick way shall we."

With that they vanished and flashed into the bedroom Serena dreaded seeing again. Savitar carried her and put her gently on the bed Serena spent so many nights crying. Saved from a hell just to be brought back into another one she thought. Savitar bit into his wrist and put it over Serena's mouth.

"Drink up kid, The strongest steel is forged by the fires of hell. Get stronger and maybe just maybe you will leave your own hell once and for all."

Serena drank all that she could. She closed her eyes thinking what her guardian had just told her. She would never get out of this hell she thought. But she made a promise to herself that she would never again be weak, she will become strong, strong enough to end all of the suffering.

"I don't want to be here right now."

"Serena don't worry, stop showing that dread. You are in my apartment. I just brought stuff from your room to make it look homey for you. Relax kid. You are safe for now. I have to take you back sooner or later, but I will be there to try to protect you, Damien as well. Get some rest I will be back for you in a few."

"Don't tell anyone else I am here ok. I died in that basement as far as anyone is concerned."

"Well, what do I call you then?"

"Jude, call me Jude."

"Why Jude?"

"I always liked the name ever since I saw that show Instant star. Don't judge me."

"Hey, Jude it is my dear. See you later.

Savitar disappeared while Serena closed her eyes, finally she was out of that hell hole and into a safe place. She wasn't safe yet Serena thought. Not until she was rid of everyone who did her wrong. She would get stronger. Strong enough to not be seen as the weak girl anymore.

Savitar found who he was looking for. He was sitting around the music shop as usual. Savitar walked up to him.

"Quincy, you are looking rather, well lets just say not well."

"Who the hell are you? Do you know what happened here?"

"You know, I am surprised at you. I was skeptical that when I learned the truth, but you have proved that you actually love her."

"Who are you? Where is Serena?"

"The only thing I can say is go to the bar, you will find your brother. Your brother knows a lot and is blabbing about it to his drunk buddies. So, go see him you will get your answer." Savitar transported away and appeared back in his apartment. He checked on Serena who was sleeping soundly. The pieces on the chess board were about to come into play and he was about to take down one of the kings of two. He was just surprised he had to use the knight so early in the game. It is up to Quincy to finish it. Savitar went to brush some strands of hair out of Serena's face. Now to help the other knight become the one thing she was always meant to be. Serena always needed to be apart of the vampire society. She never had a family to go to. Other than him that is, and Quincy. He had to find a way to get her help and into that society one way or the other, she will get out of this hell and into a peaceful existence.

CHAPTER 8

Quincy went into the bar and sat at a table behind his brother and friends. He didn't know why but he trusted that stranger who told how to find Serena. His family was after her after all.

"So, when can I see that whore again Elijah. Can we go see her tonight?"

"Relax, tomorrow night will be better tonight is torture night, she is going to be gone tonight anyway. So you need to go look for a new girl because the whore is already dead."

Quincy was furious, he couldn't believe that they used Serena like that. They were talking about her like she was nothing and like her life was nothing. The next thing he knew he went up to one of Elijah's friends and held his throat and threw him to the ground while he stabbed him in the heart. Quincy looked up to find his brother staring at him shocked. The other man tried to run but Quincy threw a knife that went in the man's heart from the back and the man went down instantly.

"Why my dear brother, do what do I give the pleasure of seeing you and stabbing two of my friends."

"Murderer."

"I don't know what you are talking about."

"Let me refresh your memory, dear brother." Quincy took his bow and arrow that he put together and shot the arrow in Elijah's thigh. "Ahhh!!! Goddammit!!!!" Elijah screamed as he sat on the bar stool.

"Anyone who interferes in this will get hurt, the bar is officially closed. Everyone out. Everyone ran out of the bar while screaming.

"Looks like it is just you and me Elijah." Quincy took a knife out and stabbed Elijah's hand. "GODAMMIT." What the fuck do you want. Why the hell are you doing this?"

"You know I have to wonder, I lost the person I ever cared about in my life, I never even got a chance to know if I was in love with her yet. I was damn close I am sure. Then without a second thought she vanished, I never saw her again."

"Maybe she realized you were a weak pathetic excuse of a man. AHHHH!" Elijah yelled while Quincy twisted the knife in his hand.

"Shh, I am the one telling the story. Anyway, I always wondered who took her, and when I got the lead on who it was, I wasn't shocked, in fact I should have realized it sooner. I can't help but wonder if my dear Serena said what you said to me. Asking why I am doing this to you. She was innocent Elijah."

"She was a fucking target."

"She didn't deserve to die."

"She did, she made you weak, father didn't like that very much. He wanted to send you a message. Oh, don't look so shocked, I saw you two one night here kissing, I told father and he told me what he wanted done the second you told him you didn't want to kill her."

"Well, brother, unfortunately my story has come to an end, father will get his in the end. I am going there after I end you. I told you both before, you know what I am capable of, you knew I would find out sooner or later, you both shouldn't have come after her. Enjoy hell."

"I will see you there." Quincy stabbed his brother in the heart. "Goodbye brother, you won't be missed, but I will make sure you won't be by yourself, Father will be joining you soon." Quincy walked out but before he could transport to his father's house someone approached him.

"That was a nice performance."

"He was a person who won't be missed."

"You're Tommy Quincy aren't you?"

"Who wants to know?"

"My name is Roman."

"You….You are the king of all the vampires. I am sorry I didn't recognize you. Excuse me for being so bold but what do you want with me?"

"It is ok, I don't like all that formal shit anyway. I wanted to bring the vampire society back together. The vampire hunters have come back. I am only bringing in the select few who were destined to be in the society to fight off the hunters. I know that you have had a tough life, I know that everyone has done you wrong. I was wondering if you wanted to fight for a good cause and not kill just for hire anymore."

"Fighting for hire is all I ever knew. It is all I am. But I left that life behind because I didn't want to do that anymore, I wanted to become a better person. I will join you, there is just one more thing I have to finish."

"By all means tie up all your loose ends. We are all meeting in New Orleans in a few weeks. I look forward to see you there."

Quincy couldn't believe it, he was destined for great things other than just killing. He never knew he was destined to protect as well. He would go to New Orleans now that there was nothing here for him anymore. He just had one more thing to do and that is to avenge the girl he ever loved.

"Guards, hurry up in here and do your job." Nick was trying to secure himself. He had just gotten word that Quincy had killed Elijah. His wife had left him. "It was a means to an end she said. You have already lost the land, it is not to far away that you loose everything because of Quincy. I will not be here when that happens." He knew that bitch just wanted his money. He had just gotten word his products and everything he has worked on was just destroyed. He had to secure himself before Quincy got to him next. Those stupid guards were not doing anything or rushing to be at his side. He heard a knock on the door.

"Finally, you people are finally doing your jobs!! Get the hell in here!!!" When the door opened a knife got thrown and hit Nick enough that it scratched his face and got thrown into the wall. Nick touched his face and felt blood from his cut. He looked up and saw Quincy standing right at the door.

"So, your guards really suck at their jobs. I took them out in twenty minutes tops. Kind of sloppy for me, but I was in a hurry to get to the vampire I really wanted."

"I don't know what you want to know but I did nothing to you."

"There, you are wrong. Trying to lie your way out of this just like Elijah. Now I will ask you calmly and won't yell since I am here. Where is she?"

"That bitch is dead, she is gone."

Quincy took a deep breath and let it out slowly. He walked up slowly to him until he got close enough to be face to face.

"You killed the only person I ever loved and only so you could teach me a lesson. Well, lesson learned." Quincy stabbed Nick in the heart and whispered in his ear. "The lesson is you screw me over and you are going to die painfully." He pulled away and walked to the door. He turned around before he left. "Have fun in hell. I think you will love it there." Quincy lit a match and threw it on Nick's desk and transported outside. He had burned his childhood home. As far as he was concerned his past. He would never forget Serena and what she meant to him. He always kept the words she always said to him, "I always learned we have three kinds of family. Those we are born to, those who are born to us, and those we let into our hearts." He lost the only family he had truly cared about. Serena. The only thing he had to remember her by was the necklace she gave him. He took one last look at his childhood home. "Goodbye Serena, may you rest easy, I have avenged you." With that said he transported to his apartment, packed a few things and went to New Orleans.

Serena woke up the next night, feeling stronger than ever. She walked into Savitar's kitchen and found him eating breakfast for him.

"How long have I been out?"

'Eh, just a day."

"Seriously. That is what you're going with here."

"Fine, a week at the most."

"What has been happening. Have my parents even figured out I was alive yet?"

"Well about that, Nick is dead, Elijah is dead, and their house burned down. If anything Klaus and Haley think you died in a burning house."

"Who the hell…"

"Well, let us not worry about that, put the past behind you. One story has closed Jude. You have to decide what you want to do now."

"Is Quincy."

"He is fine, and not returning to Long Island. He is gone. He is very nice by the way."

"What do you mean gone?"

"He is gone, vanished. Don't worry about it, I promise, in a couple of years you will see him again."

"How can you promise that."

"I am great like that. What do you want to do?"

"I want to go back."

"Really, I am surprised."

"Everyone in that house knew what they did, I want to get stronger, I almost killed myself because of every hit that they have ever given me. You are the only one who looked out for me after that. Oddly enough Damien as well. Everyone who had a part of my death needs to know what I felt. I am asking if you could teach me to fight. To defend myself. I will play the weak girl when I am back. I have a plan."

"Well, who am I to stop you. But you have to be smart about it. I will help you get stronger. It is going to take serious commitment. I will teach you sword fighting, fist fight, Anything that you can use. You will be ready to start with your revenge soon. Just promise me, If I teach you everything I know, you will let me know what you are doing and when you do it, just in case something happens I want to be able to get to you."

"I promise."

"Lets get started tonight then."

CHAPTER 9

Four year later

"Klaus, can I come in?"

"Damien, let yourself in. What do you want?"

"You have a visitor."

"Who is it, whoever it is tell them I am busy."

"Well, you will want to see this visitor, some have seen her already. I am shocked you haven't heard the rumors. It is a ghost from your past." Klaus didn't look up from his paperwork.

"Send the ghost in then."

"I am already here Klaus. Did you miss me, father?" Klaus looked up slowly. Shocked to see the last woman standing in front of him.

"Wow, the big vampire in Long Island is speechless. You are not happy to see me back from the dead?"

"How did you survive all this time?"

"I escaped from the hell you put me in. Oh, my name is Jude now just so you know."

"I can see you can change the hair and the name, but you can't change the same old dimwitted girl. You still are not the lady I thought you were."

"No, I am not the obedient daughter you want me to be."

"Guards!!!!" ten guards transported in. "Grab her, hold her still." Serena didn't struggle.

"Since you haven't learned obedience especially where I kept you for the past few years, you are going on a little trip to the woods. With no one around, by yourself. The thing is I heard you were back. It was just a matter of time when you walked your ass back to me. I also heard, you were fighting. Your mother didn't like that."

"How the hell did you hear about that?"

"I told you I have eyes everywhere. I own fucking Long Island. I have everyone in my pocket. And also our very own Damien spotted you and told me."

"You are going to be alone for four days to really think about what you want. Oh and one more thing before my dear sweet whore of a daughter goes."

"Yeah and what the hell is that?" A guard held her down on the floor. Serena tried to struggle out of his grasp but she couldn't budge.

"Something to remember the family by. I told you to hold her down. I guess this sword will have to do." AHHHH!!!!! You sick bastard!!!" Serena said as she was stabbed in the stomach, by Klaus's sword. After he stabbed her he took a branding iron with the families crest on it. "Now you will know who you belong to." AHHHHHHH!!!!!! After she was branded on her stomach the guards let her go. She was breathing hard in and out. The guards attacked her, kicked her while she could do nothing.

"Stop that is enough. We don't want to kill her boys." Klaus hunched down on his knees, and took the blade out slowly while turning it. "Since my dear late friend Nick couldn't break you, I will take a wack at." Serena couldn't speak while the guards dragged her up. "Drop her off at the Central Pine Barrens, make sure no one sees her there." After the guards left Damien walked up slowly to Klaus.

"Klaus, why the hell did you do that?"

"Well, if you must know, one she must learn her place and two someone is going to find her after she gets dropped off."

"Who?"

"Do you remember Zero, I did business with him, with Nick, and since Nick's house got burned and burned Zero's money and his shipment of humans to sell to the vampire population, he has been looking for something from me to pay him back. He did want Haley as a pay off, but I said no, Haley wouldn't do it anyway, she is my right hand, I can't loose her. Since I learned Serena is alive and well, well, lets just say she is my payoff. I just hope Zero likes his girls disobedient." Klaus said with a smile on his face. Damien left the room quickly and went to his room, making sure no one was following him on the way. He went to his phone to call Savitar. Savitar picked up on the first ring."

"Who is this and how did you get the number?"

"Savitar we have a problem."

"What? Serena didn't get in ok?"

"Worse, she got in, just not the way we planned. Klaus is pawning her off to Zero."

"Wait, What!!!!"

"He knew that she was alive, someone saw her before and fighting someone before she came back. So he already had a welcome back party waiting for her."

"Who the hell—Don't tell me you…"

"It was before you came to me ok. I still have to play two sides. You are lucky I even help you and Serena at all."

"You are lucky I let you live, you still owe me. You are lucky I am not there snatching your eyes out of their socket."

"I am sorry. What do we do now?"

"Give me where they are dropping her off, the address of Zero's place. I will take care of it."

Savitar hung up the phone and called the two people who could help her with this. Serena would get away, he knew, if Zero revealed himself. Savitar couldn't get involved himself not yet. Serena had to try to survive.

"Hello."

"It's me."

"Sav, isn't this a pleasant surprise. I haven't heard from you in a couple of years, when are you going to visit us here in New Orleans huh?"

"Soon enough. I need a favor."

"You needing a favor, I am shocked. What is it?" The woman said with amusement in her voice.

"I need you to look after someone for me. I am not supposed to be doing that. I work for her family and if they catch wind of it my plans to finally take them down are ruined. She is a good kid. I will give you an address. Watch the place for a couple of days and when you see her alone whatever state she is in, I am hoping she is fine, take her in for a bit."

"Who is she? She has to be special for you to intervene."

"Serena, she is going by Jude now."

"I hate leaving New Orleans, but if Savitar asks for a favor so be it. We will be there soon. Where are we staying?"

"I have a second apartment in Caldwell, NY, you two can stay there."

"See you." Savitar hung up, hopefully he did the right thing of not interfering now. They had a plan she wanted to stick with. Hopefully she will be ok.

CHAPTER 10

Serena was roughly dropped in the woods buy her parent's guards. They had messed her up pretty badly. She couldn't walk. This is the one variable she didn't see coming. She should have been more discrete. The only reason she attacked that vampire was because he noticed who she really was and was going to go tell her dear Klaus, since he was apart of that stupid guard detail. Serena could hardly keep her eyes opened. It is a good thing she was a halfling, she could survive during the day, if she survived the night she thought. She was trying to get up but kept falling down, she was dizzy, the last thing she saw was a figure coming toward her. She couldn't even protect herself.

Serena opened her eyes. She didn't feel the hard ground that she got thrown on, she felt a soft bed. She sat up and looked around her surroundings. She was in a lush bedroom. She was sitting on a king sized bed looking like it was from some kind of old movie. There was dark grey paint and the space was massive. She noticed that she was just in a t-shirt and a pair of men's shorts. Someone knocked on the door and walked into the room. She saw a man with silver hair and icy blue eyes. He looked both dangerous even in black suit. He also had five silver earrings. Three on his left ear cartilage and two on his right bottom.

"Welcome back to the living. I got you some blood. I know you are a vampire by seeing your teeth, but I was surprised they are shorter than expected." The stranger said putting the blood on the nightstand.

"How did I get here?"

"I saw you in the woods, I brought you to my apartment. You had passed out, you were hurt pretty badly."

"Who dressed me in this, and where are my clothes?"

"Your clothes were so ripped and torn I had to throw them away. I put you in my clothes." Serena looked at him skeptically.

"Why did you help me, you don't even know me."

"When I see a woman in trouble I help." He said smiling. "Forgive me, where are my manners, my name is Zero. And you are?"

"My name is Ser...Jude. My name is Jude. I am a halfling, so I don't need blood to survive. I can eat food like humans. Other than that I am a regular vampire." Serena got up from the bed, she looked down at her self and then looked at Zero. "How long was I out?"

"For three days."

"Well, thank you for your hospitality and your help, but I really must be going. Things to do people to see."

"You can't leave yet."

"Why is that?"

"You are still weak, you need food in you. Relax for a day. You can leave tomorrow night."

"Are you really that concerned for my well being?"

"You were badly injured, I am trying to bring you back to full health."

"I don't need to stay for another day."

"Just stay for a meal, that is all I am asking Jude. You need to be at full strength.

Serena sat down at his kitchen table and was served wine with steak and green beans. "Wow, this actually looks good. Are you not eating."

"I already ate before I came and found you awake. Dig in, it is delicious."

Serena started eating the meal and it was really good, the steak was juicy yet tender just like she liked it, and the green beans were seasoned to perfection.

"You are a really good cook, your food is delicious."

"Thank you. You should taste the wine it is extra delicious."

"I have always loved a good glass of wine." Serena took a couple of sips of wine and continued eating. When she was done she stood up. "Thank you for the food and the wine. Everything was spectacular. Especially the wine. Where did you get it, I may buy some for me."

"It is something I made personally."

"You should import it. You could make a fortune off this. Is that what you do, make wine?"

"Something like that. Everyone tells me I should sell it." There was a knock on the door.

"Excuse me."

"Hey Zero, where is this girl you told us so much about. I don't care what we have to do even if it means sharing with this lot." They all laughed.

"All in due time gentlemen. Just wait in the bedroom. I will be right there." Frowning, Serena didn't find anything funny about that man's comments. She didn't feel safe here anymore, so she tried to find some excuse to leave and quickly. All of a sudden Serena felt a calm peace she had ever known that settled over her, like she was sleeping while awake. She felt warm and hot, and dizzy She automatically went to the floor. Zero came up behind her.

"Don't fight it Serena." Serena couldn't talk, how did he know her real name. She felt so hot. She tried to walk to the door but she fell.

"How did you know my name?"

"Oh, in due time you will know." Zero moved to sit behind her, and moved her so she was laying on her back in front of him. Serena tried to get up, but Zero held her down. Before Serena could get up her hands were pinned above her head. Zero ripped the clothes off her body.

Ze...Zero what are you doing?" Zero pulled down his pants and laid on top of Serena.

"I am getting what I was promised. Your father did give me permission to do what I want with you. He didn't tell me how pretty you were. I have seen pictures of you, but never imagined I would ever get the real thing. I intend to savor taking you for hours to come."

Serena came to, her head spinning, she tried her best to focus as Zero and his friends talked in the bedroom.

"Who is next to have her?" Zero looked at Serena, feeling him lick her throat. "You are about to learn lesson number two my dear Serena. You can never get away from me. You have already been here for six weeks." Serena passed out again.

CHAPTER 11

Serena woke up, with a clear head. Every place on her body was sore. She looked around and no one was in the room. All the days have been running together. The last thing she remember was Zero saying she had been there for six weeks. No telling what they had been doing. Serena trembled. She heard someone open the door, when the lights came on she saw Zero with a smile on his face.

"No memory, it is amazing what I have learned in my lifetime as a vampire, what kind of drugs I can mix together and put into drinks. Even though you have been with so many men on and off, you have no memory. You will regain it eventually bit by bit, which would be fun to see the look on your face when you do remember. The third lesson is, I own you now. Your father gave you to me. But you will be a willing participant in the activities. I can have you begging me to take you so easily."

"Fuck you!"

"Aww my dear Serena, you already have plenty of times. I need my rest. Maybe one more time before I rest next to you." Zero rushed to her side and grabbed the wine and poured it down her throat. Serena almost choked it out. Zero waited for a few minutes and Serena passed out again.

Serena woke up groggy, she couldn't believe this was happening. she looked and felt around. Zero was laying next to her while she was cuffed to the bed. There was a little light coming from the blinds. It was morning. It would hurt but she could go out during the day. She looked around to look for something that will help her pick the lock. she saw a small pin on the night stand. She picked it up, it took her a few minutes, but she got herself unshackled. She got up from the bed then fell, her legs felt so weak. She got back up and looked for something to cover her up. She just found a t-shirt and put that on. She wanted to get out of here as soon as possible. She shackled Zero to the bed so he couldn't follow her and took the lamp and smashed it on his head. "That should knock him out for a few hours." she thought to herself. She wanted to kill him for what he did to her, but all in due time. Serena walked out of the apartment and into the early morning. The sun is just coming up. She didn't know where she was so she just started walking until she got somewhere familiar. Suddenly a car pulled up right next to her driving slowly to keep up with her pace. The man rolled down the window. He had short messy brown hair, with brown eyes. He had warm eyes as he looked calm and tranquil. But it seemed like if he had to he could protect himself. He was dressed down in a red t-shirt, blue jeans, and a black leather jacket.

"So, you are the mysterious girl I should look after." Serena kept walking ignoring the stranger.

"I guess I understand the cold shoulder treatment, but I can't understand how a pretty girl like you is just dressed in a t-shirt with nowhere else to go."

"Leave me the fuck alone."

"Wow, feisty, I love it." The stranger said while laughing.

"My wife would like you, better yet I shouldn't introduce you two. Two witty people are enough."

"I will hurt you if you don't go."

"Well, I can't. You look weak, even for a halfling. You should get out of the sun, you don't look like you need a tan." When Serena stopped in her tracks the man stopped as well.

"How the hell does a human like you know whether or not I am a halfling."

"Well, I will tell you my secrets if you tell me yours."

"It doesn't matter, you can move along now."

"You see that is where you are wrong, I can't just go. I am supposed to follow you."

"Leave!"

"So the story is Serena, yes I know your name. My wife gets a call in the middle of the night. We are all the way in New Orleans, about to get ready for a club opening, and one of our oldest friends calls up and asks for a favor. We can't say no, He has done so much for us and vice versa. I have lost count on who owes who now. Anyway, he says to look after a girl named Serena, a.k.a. Jude Harrison. Described you and here we are."

"How did you find me?"

"Well, he gave an address he said wait until you came out. He thought you would be out sooner than this. He will be very shocked that it took you a month to get out. He was rather worried about you."

"A month!!" I have been in—"Serena couldn't believe it, but she had to, with that stuff that Zero had been giving her he even said she would have no memory and that weeks had past last time she just couldn't imagine regaining the memory, she hoped she never would.

"Are you ok, what happened in there?" The stranger looked at her with concern in his eyes.

"Don't worry about it."

"You are very strong, I wonder who do you talk to when everything becomes too much?"

"Not you. So leave me be."

"I told you already I can't. Once I set out to do something I see it through."

"Why should I trust you huh? I don't even know you."

"Well, I guess I should drop his name, he said to if you didn't believe me or my girl. The person who sent us all the way from New Orleans is Savitar."

Serena laughed. "I don't believe you."

"Savitar, the same person who saved you after cutting yourself in your room, ever since that day he vowed to be your guardian ever since. Try to get to you wherever you are and keep track of you to make sure you are ok. You vowed revenge on your parents Klaus and Haley. Who I already hate by the way. Need I go on?"

"Why did Savitar send you and he didn't come. I have been stuck in there for a month and he didn't come!"

"He couldn't go in you and I both know that. He does protect you yes, but he does work for your parents. It is dangerous to go against them when you two have the plan that you do. That is why he sent us, but we didn't know the situation in there that is why we didn't burst in there. I am sorry. Savitar didn't know anything that was happening in there either. He has been out on your father's behalf. Messing up things on the inside. He is looking out for you.

He sent us to help you, I promise, I know that people have let you down and you have met nothing but assholes but please trust us. Get in the car and you will be safe. Plus my wife and I will teach you more things to help with your fighting, like how to shoot bow and arrows. That would be fun huh." He said with a smile. Serena laughed. "I got to make you laugh, that just made my day. So how about it. Coming?"

Serena went around to the passenger side and got in the car.

"There we go. Lets start a new fun chapter."

"You know my name, yet I don't know yours."

"My name is Kieren, my wife is Trista, or trist for short. You will meet her when we get to Caldwell."

"Caldwell, NY, why there?"

"It is the only place we could go, on short notice. Savitar's apartment is there. We are staying there."

"Well, I really trust you now. A lot of people don't know about that place. He really trust you two."

"We are good friends. Why don't we stop somewhere and get you some clothes and then something to eat and then we will go to Caldwell."

"Sounds good."

"Awesome."

CHAPTER 12

Serena and Kieren finally arrived at the apartment in Caldwell. It was much bigger than the apartment in Long Island. When they walked inside she noticed that the apartment had two floors. It was big.

"Wow, I wish I had an apartment like this."

"Right, my apartment only has one floor."

"Kieren, is that you. Is it my turn to steak out the place, I know how tired you are why don't you— Who is this?"

"Trist meet Serena well, I am sorry, Jude. Jude meet my wife Trista." Trista walked up to her and smiled. She had dark long flowing black hair with dark brown eyes. She looked like a goddess in her purple skirt, black blouse and purple heels.

"Oh, hey, I was wondering when I was going to meet the girl who made the great Savitar ask for a favor." Trista said that with amusement in her voice.

"That's him, always does things alone." They all laughed.

"Take a seat Jude, relax, you are definitely safe for now. Would you like something to eat?"

"Did you cook it?"

"Odd question to ask. Why do you ask?"

"I have bad experience with someone cooking me food."

"Ah, well, no. it is takeout. Chinese food. Some egg rolls and fried rice, and lo mein."

"Um sure then. Thank you."

"Eh, you don't have to thank us. You are our friend now." Serena frowned at that word. She never had a lot of friends. Everyone has just betrayed her at ever turn. It was only a matter of time before these two just left her out in the cold.

"I hear you dance. So do I."

"I haven't danced for years."

"We cleared a space if you want to do it again. I have always wanted a dance partner. I mean Kieren dances, but he is not that good between you and me."

"I am literally right here honey."

"Love you." Trista said with a smile.

"Uh Huh." Seeing Trista and Kieren banter like this and being friendly and loving, made Jude sad, she wishes that someone had been that way with her.

"So Jude, I hear that you have started learning how to fight. What can you do?"

"Savitar taught me some fist fighting, sword fighting, that is about it so far."

"He left the rest of the weapons to us, so it would seem. He knows who is the best at it."

"You better not let Sav hear that Trist, he might just do a little contest to prove who is the best."

"Bring it on." Trista said while laughing.

"He asked you two to train me?"

"Yeah, but it seems from what he already told us you know a lot. All you are missing is more weapons, and a little more fighting with your fist and a lot of kicking. The thing I can give you, is knife throwing, and shooting a bow and arrow. That I can say Savitar is better at than me."

"So, when do you want to get started. I was thinking this weekend. We can relax until then get some food. Explore Caldwell. What do you say."

"Um…I don't know."

"Oh come on we don't bite much. Hang out with us. It has been a while since we just relaxed for a bit. We have been mostly working."

"Where do you guys work?"

"This crazy man of mine decided to open a club in New Orleans near the french Quarter."

"Oh you love it. You can dance and sing whenever you want."

"True, so true. Do you sing Jude?"

"A little. I have always loved to sing and dance, but that is a long time ago. I also play the piano. I have always wanted to learn how to play the guitar. Ever since I saw a show, A gibbson actually. It looked so pretty, and so awesome."

"Interesting. it seems we all have a lot in common. This is the start of a beautiful friendship."

CHAPTER 13

Six Year Later
Present

"Ok Jude just like we practiced, shoot your target." Serena brought the arrow up and focused on the bullseye in front of her. When she shot it she got the arrow in the center. After that she quickly put the bow down got her knives and threw all of them at the center of the dummy hanging next to her. She then faced Kieren. Kieren came at her and tried to punch him in the face, she dodged it and tried to punch him back but he stepped back. They circled around each other both trying to feel out the other's next move. Kieren moved forward and kicked Serena, but she ducked down, Serena tried to sweep his legs from under him but he jumped up. Jude then got up and kicked Kieren in the stomach which made him loose his balance a bit and step back. Jude then swept his legs got her knife and sat on top of him while holding a knife to his throat. They were both breathing hard.

"Congratulations you just graduated." Kieren said smiling. Jude smiled and got up.

"Am I really good enough, or are you just saying that to make me feel better?"

"Hey, you got past me, you can get past any person who tries to come at you. I would say you are deadly. Which is appropriate, you do have someone in mind you want to kill."

"A couple of people actually."

"Right. So you are ready to be dropped in the real world. Are you ready to go back and face the leeches?"

"No, but I have to sometime."

"Trista, get in here." Trista walked in with a big box in her hands and dropped it in front of Jude.

"What is this?"

"We hope to see you again in the near future soon, but in the mean time the two of us decided to get you a going away present."

"Well, presents"

"Why would you do this?"

"Jude, the three of us, have had fun together this whole time and hung out, despite everything that has gone on in your life we are your friends, and you are stuck with us and all that mushy blah blah."

"Yeah, that mushy blah blah." Jude said to herself. Jude smiled, for the first time in a long time, she was happy that she met kieren and Trista, she knew that they were friends. Jude opened the box, when she finally opened it and looked inside, she looked up stunned.

"Yo, you got me a gibson guitar, and a sword."

"Well, I didn't teach you how to play guitar for nothing, Also the sword was Savitar's, he wanted you to have it. He even had it in scripted look. Jude looked at the sword and read the inscription "The strongest steel is forged by the fires of hell" "That is what he said to me when he rescued me from Nick."

"Thank you guys for everything, I am glad I met you two."

"Come see us on your weekend breaks huh. Just be careful, ok. Your father is smart."

"I will Trist."

"In a few seconds I will hug you, are we good with that?"

"I hate hugs."

"Hugging you anyway." Jude was hesitant, but hugged Trista back.

"Call us if you ever need our help. Your father knows by now that you are out and about, and he is pissed. He also found out about you killing that guard in that new outfit of yours. What is with that outfit anyway?"

"There has been a rumor going on, not a lot of people know if I am really alive or not, there is a reason Klaus hasn't told anyone I am alive. According to Damien he wants to use me to put fear in his vampire buddies. That is what I sent a message with Damien saying that I will do it, if he pays me and he leaves me the hell alone. I will be the dutiful daughter he always wanted. Everyone thinks I am a ghost, they don't think I am real, I am good at this."

"Huh, so you are an assassin now for your ass of a father. That can't go wrong."

"I am fine. You don't understand, I feel nothing. You both have been so nice and I feel nothing. I feel cold. I am good at this. I have become cold and calculating."

"If you need help call us that is all I am saying."

"Fine, I will."

"Jude, being cold is always fun, but one day you won't be as cold."

"I hope you're right. I have to go. Apparently I have to go see Klaus in person for this job. He wants me to personally handle this one."

"Good luck, hey, at least you are killing cruel vampires right."

"Yeah, see you."

"Later." Trista took Kieren's hand and they transported back to New Orleans. She knew she would never be the happy girl she was again. Klaus wanted to break her, he succeeded. Now the only thing to know was who would win in the end, her, or them. Jude took her guitar and sword and transported to her childhood bedroom. She went into the hallway and found Damien walking to his room.

"There she is. I feel like I haven't seen you in years."

"Well, I have been busy."

"Of course, killing off Klaus's competition. Along with the people who stand against him. People think you are some kind of ghost, a boogieman."

"They should. I am a person's worse nightmare. Where is he?"

"Dining hall with Haley. There is another guest, but everyone loves a good surprise, and this one Jude, will make you want to just burn the house down. Good luck." Jude transported to outside the dining hall. She couldn't figure out who this guest is. One way to figure it out she thought. She opened the door and saw Klaus and Haley at the head of the table of course. The special guest had his back to her.

"Serena, welcome back, you are finally out of hiding are you?"

"Well, after you begged me to come see you how could I refuse you mother."

"Why is it when you say mother it sounds like an insult?"

"Well, I think it is." Jude said smiling. "What did you two want."

"Patience patience. All in due time. There are two things. One you left something behind you were not supposed to. I believe you are owned by someone other than me. And two this person that you left behind got the job for you."

"Long time no see my dear Serena." Jude recognized that voice right away. She could never forget it. Why did he has to be here, she thought she had been rid of him when she left him six years ago. Zero stood up looking as formal as ever. Only this time he had a cold look in his eyes.

"I told you, you can't run from me."

"Well, then I guess I got one hell of a head start then since you haven't been able to find me. What is the job?" Zero walked up to her and slapped her.

"You know I used to love your witty tongue now, I despise it and need you to get rid of it."

"What is the job. That is all I came here for."

"Did you not here me, I can make your life a living hell or did you forget." Zero got close to whisper in her ear. "I can get to you whenever I feel like, you are mine. I can make you beg whenever I feel like it, so you will show me respect. Do you hear me?"

"Understood." Jude couldn't afford to get Zero angry. As much as she hated him she hated what he could do more. Zero handed her two pictures. "The job is that man and woman. You need to kill them."

"What did they do?"

"Who the hell cares, do you always need an explanation before your kills."

"They look human."

"Who cares they need to die, do it or you die. Take your pick."

"Fine, what is the deadline?"

"Four days."

"Fine, can I go now."

"Leave, but after you are done come back here, so I know the job is done."

"Fine." Jude walked out. For the most part she hasn't been killing humans, just vampires. "Something is not right about this," she thought. She called the only person who could find out.

"What?"

"You sound busy."

"Hey kid, long time no talk. What did you need?"

"I need your help."

"A little tied up at the moment."

"Hmm, if I know you like I think I do, you are tied up by having a girl over and entertaining her with your skills."

"Ah you do know me well. Fine, hold on." Jude held on but could hear the conversation. "You need to leave."

"You are just kicking me out."

"I am going to be busy, I will call you."

"You don't have my number."

"I can read your mind I got your number." Jude heard a door slam.

"You know you can't really read minds right?"

"Eh, whatever she was a little boring. So, what can I do for you?"

"I need some info on two people I am supposed to be killing. I don't know what it is about these two but something isn't right."

"Could it be you just don't want something to be right. You just want everything to be wrong."

"Why would I do that?"

"I have been keeping an eye on you kid, you have gotten pretty hesitant on your targets for the past few weeks. I saw that you got cut."

"I was giving them a fighting chance."

"You don't give chances. What is going on?"

"Nothing, please Sav, don't push too much on it."

"Fine, I will call in a few with some results." Jude hung up. She went back to her room and opened the envelope to read some of the usual information on her targets. Where they are, what they do. Apparently they were in New Orleans. Looks like she was seeing Kieren and Trista sooner than she thought.

CHAPTER 14

Jude arrived in New Orleans. She rented an apartment a few blocks away from her targets. She had just finished unpacking when she heard the front door open. She went into hiding real quick and grabbed one of her knives. The person who had broke in was running for the front door when Jude threw a knife that hit her shirt to stop her from leaving. She walked out from hiding to approach the person who broke in when she saw it was a teenage girl, her target.

"Hey, seriously, you ruined a perfect jacket." The girl pulled the knife out of her jacket.

"How did you get in."

"The door was opened."

"No, it wasn't. I locked it."

"It was unlocked." Serena went to jiggle the door knob, the lock was broken.

"Are you the new owner of this place. I knew the last owners they let me in here all the time."

"What did you steal?"

"I didn't steal any—ow." Jude grabbed her hand and found the locket that Quincy had given her with his picture in it.

"Please don't tell my dad."

"Fine, please go." The girl rushed out of the house. Jude wanted to forget everything for a while. She went for a walk.

"Excuse me have you seen a girl with long brown hair down her back, with goldish brown eyes, 5 foot 4." Jude turned around to see a man on her door step.

"You mean the girl who broke into my place."

"I am sorry about that. We just knew the last owners of this apartment. You just rented this place right?"

"Yeah I did."

"Oh I am sorry, my name Vince Tyler." Vince put out his hand, but when Serena didn't shake his hand in return he pulled it back.

"My name is Jude, nice to meet you."

"Well, welcome to the french quarter. Hopefully my daughter didn't cause too much trouble. I will see you around." Vince walked away. Jude saw the second target. "Interesting, they are father and daughter," she thought. She put that thought out of her head, they were targets after all she had to get this done and leave as soon as possible.

The next night Jude took her guitar case up to the roof close to the apartment Vince and that girl lived. She opened up and took out the guitar and put together her bow and arrow. She was ready. Looking through her microscope so she can get a close up and hit her targets. For some reason she was hesitant, she couldn't do it. She stood there frozen for a couple of minutes until she put down the arrow. "Dammit," she thought. She had no idea why she was having problems with this. She packed up and went home.

The next morning Jude got a phone call from Damien.

"Serena Zero is getting impatient, this is the longest you ever took on a job."

"Just tell him I need a few more days."

"I will try, he is getting really impatient, either you do it or he will send someone else to kill them and to come get you." Damien hung up. Jude was frustrated, she went outside to sit on her steps. That girl showed up in front of her.

"Why did you tell my dad I broke in?"

"Because you did."

"Well, he grounded me for it. He even wanted me to invite you to dinner."

"That is ok."

"Come on please, usually it is just me and my dad, sometimes it drives me a bit crazy." Jude breathed out slowly and walked back up the steps. She paused. "Fine what time?"

"8 sharp. My name is Holly Tyler by the way. What is yours?"

"Jude." With that Jude went inside the apartment.

Jude couldn't believe that Savitar hadn't called yet. She needed to know about who these people are. For some reason there was something about those two that she couldn't go through with it. She had to warn them tonight and get them out damn the consequences. She got to their house. When she got in the building she found some of the guards from Klaus's detail waiting for them. She looked around to see if anyone was there. She ran up to the one on the side and stabbed him from behind. And then stepped to the one on the stairs and took her knife out and stabbed the man in the heart. She waited until the vampires vanished, so she could knock on the door.

Vince opened the door looking surprised to find Jude there.

"Jude what are you."

"I thought I was invited?" Vince and Jude both looked at holly who looked mischievous.

"I will just go now."

"No, It is fine, please come in." Jude walked into their apartment. She had to figure out what was going on. She suddenly saw a shadow outside. She missed one. Probably back up in case those two guys failed. "Vince, go take Holly and hide."

"What are you—"

"GO NOW!!" As soon as Jude said that the guy broke in through the window. Vince and Holly went to hide in his room. Jude took out her knife and threw it at the man but he dodged it. She ran to him and punched him in the face, she managed to get him to the ground and put his own knife to his throat.

"Why does Zero want them so badly?"

"You have failed. Zero will send more until you do what you were set out to do."

Jude stabbed him in the heart. When Jude got up she saw Vince and Holly standing there shocked.

"Who are you!?"

"Doesn't matter. What the hell did you two do?"

"We didn't do anything."

"You had to, one of you. Did you see something you weren't supposed to or what? Forget it, you two come with me, we are going to my place."

CHAPTER 15

When Jude, Vince, and Holly got back to her apartment, she saw Savitar sitting in the living room waiting for her.

"Wow, I am surprised. She actually saved you two. Do you know what she does for a living?"

"Savitar what did you figure out?"

"Well, these two humans, saw an exchange go on between Zero himself and your old friend Catherine getting some humans to give to a couple of vampires. Apparently they saw them tasting the product. They ran and hid. You remember Catherine don't you?"

"The bitch was Nick's wife. She left. Why is she in this?"

"She is with Zero now." She persuaded Zero to send people after them."

"Dad how did they know that?"

"I know a lot."

"You have to do something Savitar. Zero is already getting impatient."

"It is not Zero who is getting impatient it is Catherine. She is in New Orleans even. Lives in the Garden District, big house with neighbors so far away from her."

"Did this girl tell you she is half vampire and what she was sent to do?"

"You are a vampire, I knew it. I knew they were vampires."

"Forget it, it is whatever."

"Wait." Jude paused when she was about to walk outside. She turned to Vince.

"We don't care what you are what you were sent to do, you have been nice to us. Helped us and you didn't need to."

"I came to kill you two, that is what I am doing here. Still like me."

"But you didn't."

"What?"

"You didn't. You could have."

"Sav—." Savitar had already left. Damn him but he knew what she already knew. She was done after they found out about this. It was time that she left for good and begin her revenge.

"I will help you. But you need to stay hidden. There is a place in Caldwell, NY. Change your names, your habits, what you do. I will check on you from time to time and make sure you are ok. This place is yours. Pack and leave now."

"What are you going to do?"

"Start a war."

"Thank you, for helping us."

"Yeah Yeah. Just make sure you go." Vince and Holly left quickly. Jude went upstairs and unpacked an outfit that she would wear one last time she hoped. She put on a black leather bustier with matching black leather pants with black boots that came up to her calves. Along with her guitar pic necklace and the locket that Quincy gave her, showing off her infinity tattoo on her wrist, and her serpentine bracelet.

Serena put on her long black hooded coat to hide her outfit and went to see Kieren and Trista.

Jude hopped off her silver Suzuki hayabusa motorcycle in front of Kieren's club and went to see her two friends. It was crowded for the party tonight, as she went in. When Jude went to sit down at the bar, Trista walked straight over after serving a group of guys their drinks.

"Hey Jude, you decided to come to this party willingly. I don't imagine you are going to dance or sing will you?" Trista said with a smile.

"No, I won't sing, and you know why I don't anymore, but if you need another dancer then I am yours to command."

"Haha, well well, I didn't think that we could get the great big scary Jude to dance. You owe me ten dollars Trist."

Jude looked behind the bar to see Kieren standing there with a big smile on his face.

"Oh so we are betting on me now, I get it I have been MIA lately but I am here right. Does that count for anything?"

"Well, maybe just in your terms, but since we didn't have to come find you, you get some points and you you have to dance."

"Fine just say when and I will dance, but I am not changing into any costumes."

"Deal. "Trista said smiling.

Trista gave a beer to Jude while she walked away to take more orders from other customers.

"You know Kierien this is my last night here before I have to go back to New York. You two could be a little sentimental for me."

"Ha, the day you want sentiment from us is the day that I will put on a dress for one week and shave my head bald."

Serena laughed

"I will remember that, that is actually a weird visual. The next time I need something because I am sad I will first come to you and say I what dress you are going to wear.

"Ha Ha, very funny. I am going to do my rounds, do you need me before I go?"

"No I am good, go take care of your customers, I am not staying long anyway. I still need to pack. I am only going to stay for one dance, so tell Trist to make it a good song."

"She only knows the best songs. Later."

Jude sat at the bar when Aimee put a glass of wine in front of her. Jude looked up at Aimee puzzled.

"That man two seats down sent it. I would take the invitation." She said winking and walked away.

Jude looked and she couldn't believe her eyes, she could hardly breathe. All the guy had to do is look at her she thought. That is all he had to do to confirm her suspicions. When he finally looked up those brown eyes that had haunted her dreams time and time again. Same eyes same face same calm cool look as when they first met all those years ago. Quincy walked over to her with the look of recognition on his face.

Quincy looked around the club. This is the first break he had in a couple of years. He couldn't believe how long it has been since he left New York. He had gotten use to New Orleans and the atmosphere. Still he always carried a piece of his past with him. The necklace Serena had given him. When he was going to the bar he paused, that woman talking to that man and woman, she looked so familiar to him. She just had to turn around real quick and she did. A petite slender build and brown eyes. Dark brown hair down to her back with a lighter golden brown highlighted in her beautiful hair with mixed auburn strands that caught the light. She was wearing a long black coat with short sleeves, and black thigh boots. He wondered what she was wearing under that. But he didn't care. She looked so familiar to him. Like they knew each other once upon a time. She looked like...He couldn't do that to himself. Serena died a few years ago. He decided to send her a drink. When he noticed that she may have accepted it, he went up to her.

"Do I know you from somewhere?"

She breathed out slowly, thankful that he didn't recognize her. Her past life was done, she didn't want the past to come back, especially with the man who hurt her.

"No, you don't, you are mistaken."

"Huh, my apologies then, I thought you were someone I knew."

"No worries about it. So if that is it, I would like to get back to being by myself now."

"You know this may seem weird but I found myself drawn to you."

"Well you shouldn't I am a mess after all. You should go back and find someone new.

"Where are my manners, let me introduce myself. I am Tommy Quincy. People call me Quincy. And you are?"

"Hmm, do you really think you can get my name, I am not that easy."

"Challenged accepted then mystery girl. By the end of the night if I have not gotten your name by any means accident or not I get a kiss and a conversation."

Jude smiled. Quincy was the same as ever, he was the smooth talker he always was. She wished she could get close to him again but it was too dangerous to get close to anyone right now.

"Your on Tommy."

"Quincy, you can call me Quincy."

"Yet Tommy sounds so much better."

"Fine, for you only Tommy it is."

"Don't I just feel all special and warm inside."

Quincy, couldn't believe it, he hasn't felt this relaxed with someone since talking with Jude. Something about this woman was so familiar.

"Oh, by the end of the night you will fall in love with me."

"Ha, it is that simple huh."

"Yes it is."

"Jude, we got a dance number, Our own version of Toxic, do you remember it."

Dammit, Serena thought, Trista always had bad timing.

"Yeah, Trist I remember, but I can't tonight."

"Oh come on, it is a quick version, you know that and it will be fun to have the unholy trinity together again. you, me, Aimee.

"I can't, I have other plans."

Trista left to get to the stage. "I will be right back."

"So Jude the singer and dancer. That is quite the talent."

"You don't even know the half of it. I guess you won the bet huh."

"I think you owe me something" Quincy said whispering in Jude's ear.

Jude felt shivers going down her spine. Jude went up close and up to his ear.

"Later perhaps, I have some business to take care of"

Jude walked off to join Aimee and Trista on stage.

"Quincy we need to go, I found some vampire slayers close to the french quarter."

"I will meet you there Dante, I have one thing to take care of first."

"Jude, what is going on?"

"I have one more thing I have to do here. My fun is over for the time being."

"What do you mean."

"I have to face an old enemy of mine. Catherine. She is in town and after a couple of innocents."

"I thought you were only here to kill two targets." Kieren said with concern in his voice.

"Oh no, this is rich, the two targets are the innocent humans aren't they?" Trista said with a smile.

"Whatever I need to take care of it."

"I never thought I would see the day where the coldhearted assassin Jude would actually care."

"I don't, they were just innocent and saw something they weren't supposed to. They shouldn't die because of that." Kieren and Trista both laughed.

"What!?"

"It is nothing, Do what you need to."

CHAPTER 16

After Jude finished talking to Trista about what was going on she went to the entrance to leave. She had to get back before she had a hunting party for her. She said her good byes to Trista and Kieren.

"Be careful Jude, make sure you watch your back, and if you need our help you call us."

"I will Kieren thanks. I will see you in a couple of months or earlier if I am lucky."

Jude was outside about to walk back to her apartment when someone grabbed her arm gently. Serena turned around to find Quincy.

"I am glad I caught you Jude, you weren't just going to leave without saying goodbye were you?"

"Sorry Quincy something urgent came up I got to go."

"Wait, when can I see you again?"

Jude just looked in his eyes, she wanted to walk into his arms and stay there where she always felt safe, but she couldn't not anymore.

"I am not sure."

Quincy took her phone and put his number in it.

"Just in case you get sure sometime, you have my number."

"You are just so sure of yourself aren't you?"

"Haha, I am just confident. I feel like we have known each other forever. What is that on your arm?"

"Oh, something someone close to me always said, that stuck by me."

"What are they?" Quincy asked curiously.

"Umm…I always learned we have three kinds of family. Those we are born to, those who are born to us, and those we let into our hearts. I live by those words."

"And the infinity symbol at the end."

"Oh, someone I used to know, I told them I would love them infinity times infinity. It stuck with us. I lost him. So this reminds me of him."

"I am sorry."

"It is ok. I know I will find someone who will be in my heart again."

Quincy turned serious while looking at her, he walked up closely to her and kissed her. The past crept up on her the second he kissed her. It felt so familiar. HIs kiss was so fierce and hot yet still tender. She was breathing in the familiar spicy scent of his skin. Oh how she wanted to tell him her real identity, but she didn't have the heart to do it. There was no point of going back to that place in her past especially with how her life was now. One day perhaps but not again. All too soon he broke the kiss.

"I will see you soon I hope Jude."

Quincy walked away. Jude was happy but at the same time disappointed that he didn't remember her. No reason to dwelt on it, it is not like she would ever see him again. But why did the sound of that hurt her so much. Jude looked around and saw no one around. She She walked back to her motorcycle to go start something that would end her.

Jude finally got to Catherine's house, she parked outside the gate. The guard recognized her right away.

"You are not allowed in you whore." Jude finally recognized him as one of the men Zero let in. Jude flashed to his side and stabbed him, he went down instantly. She saw an intercom to talk to different rooms in the house. She located an intercom to Catherine's room she pressed the button.

"Hello Catherine."

"Who is this, you are not the usual guard."

"I am surprised you don't recognize the girl you and your husband tortured for a few years, but then again I guess it has been a while."

"Serena, to what do I owe this displeasure."

"You sent me after two humans who saw you and Zero doing some business. You told Zero to send me to kill them. I am telling you to leave it be."

"You didn't kill them, they saw us, they could expose us."

"Don't worry about them."

"I knew you were weak, you should have been keeping an eye on them."

"What the hell are you talking about?"

"Jude, just le—"

"You have them." Dammit she thought, she should have kept them with her.

"Let them go now."

"Sorry dear, they are already dead. Zero gave me the go ahead. Also for insubordination I have been given the go ahead to kill you." Jude couldn't think. Everyone who ever got close to her only got into trouble. She couldn't believe Holly and Vince were dead. She wasn't able to protect them. Jude stood up with an angry look.

"Catherine, look out your window." Catherine looked out her window and saw Jude.

"Hmph, now I now where you are, stay right there. I am coming up." Jude destroyed the intercom with her knife.

"Guards hurry up down to the first floor. You two follow me and guard the door to my room." Catherine walked up the steps and into her room to make a phone call.

"Zero, it is me. You need to come get me, Serena didn't kill those two humans I had to get my hands dirty. She is coming to kill me, and soon I think you are all next too."

"Oh my dear Catherine you are just a means to an end. I didn't need you anymore anyway. Those two stupid humans are all I needed to do to get Serena there. You helped my plan."

"That is why you handed those humans over to me, you bastard!!"

"Good bye Catherine." Zero hung up. Hopefully her guards were strong enough to hold off Serena and kill her once and for all.

Jude walked up to the house and got the door open. When she got to the living room she stopped and found ten guards waiting for her in front of the steps.

"Now before we start this does anyone want to leave?" All the guards pulled out weapons, while Jude just stood there. They all rushed toward her. Jude blocked the first person who came caught him in a choke hold, all the guards stopped and one came at her as she kicked the guy she was holding toward him. Jude threw a couple of knives at four of them who went down. She kicked two guys who came close to her and took out her sword. She got two guys in one swing. She dodged another who tried to stab her by ducking down and sweeping the legs right from under him and stabbed him with her sword, while throwing two knives at two more guards. When she finally finished off the last guard she went up the steps. It was quiet in the hallway until she saw a tall guard standing in front of a door at the end of the hallway. That must be where Catherine is she thought. Jude was walking up to the guy and stopped and turned slightly to see another man in front of the stairwell. When she turned the other man was gone and so was the guy near the stairwell. She kept walking until one of them appeared and jumped up and tried to kick her. She dodged it with her hands while stepping back, he kept trying to kick her but blocked every blow. She tried to punch back but he dodged it with his hands. He tried to kick her in the stomach but she grabbed his leg the other guy appeared to kicked her forward then disappeared. The other guy appeared again and kicked her on the side of her head. she pushed him backwards with a kick, while he came back and jumped kicked her in the face, she got pushed back and the other man kicked her forwards. The other man kicked her to the ground. Jude looked around to find the other man, and looked at the man in front of her. She was signaling for him to come to her, then he signaled her to come to him. The man finally came to her to kick her but she rolled out of the way. She jumped up and the man tried to kick her but she dodged it. She got in a few punches and pushed the man back. She signaled with her hands for the man to come to her, then he signaled for her to come to him. The man tried to kick her but she dodged it. She kicked him in the face. The other man kicked her and made her step back. The other guy who she was fighting reappeared and tried to kick her, but she grabbed his foot. He backflipped and Jude managed to grab his legs and make him land upside down on his neck breaking it in the process. The other man reappeared and ran at her, with a knife he managed to get Jude in the stomach and kicked her backwards. He tried to ax kick her but she rolled out of the way. she took her knife and threw it in his heart. He went down. She threw a knife at the other vampire and to make him fully disappear. Jude got up slowly and walked up to the door limping. Jude opened the door to find Catherine holding a gun to Holly's head, she saw Vince on the floor dead.

"So you didn't kill both of them after all."

"Well I stabbed her in the leg, you know what that is like. I needed her for collateral damage against you." Jude walked toward them, but Catherine pointed the gun closer to Holly's head.

"I am disappointed in you, instead of doing what you are told like a good girl you are doing all this useless running around."

"Well you know, I don't like to waste anytime."

"Me either, and I find you a big waste of time."

"Wait, if you kill that girl, I will have all the time to kill you." Catherine was about to pull the trigger when Jude threw a knife at her hand. Jude threw another knife and stabbed Catherine in the thigh making her go down to the ground. Holly got up and ran behind Jude. Jude gave her her car keys. "Holly drive my bike, to my friend' Kyrien and Trista's house in the french quarter the address is plugged into the gps which is on the bike. Tell them I sent you. They will take care of you."

"What about you?"

"Go, I will be there soon." Holly hugged Jude and ran quickly out of there. Jude walked up to Catherine.

"Wow, how the mighty have fallen."

"I am not afraid of you, you bitch."

"You should be, enjoy the fires of hell Catherine, I hear it is nice for criminals like you this time of year." Jude broke her neck and stabbed her. After Jude killed Catherine, she flashed out of the house and started limping down the street. She couldn't go back to the apartment she rented, they would be looking for her there. First she had to find some kind of shelter. While she was walking she heard a noise. As she walked toward it and got closer she heard a man scream. She hid behind a wall and saw the most craziest wonderful thing that she ever saw. At first glance she thought it was just men being macho and fighting for no reason other than to prove that they can fight. When she looked closer, she noticed that the men who were fighting were not what they seemed, while they were fighting some of the men just disappeared and she heard the words vampire and we will kill all you blood sucking creatures. Jude looked a little closer and saw that a few of the men were in trouble of being a cobob. If she didn't help they were about to be done for. Jude looked down she was in no state to fight, but she had to help. With hesitancy she crouched down and opened her guitar case and lifted up the guitar and she put together her bow and arrow. When she came back up with good precision she aimed the arrow at the man who had the guy pinned down on the ground. With a silent breath that she let out she looked up, aimed, and shot at the man, and hit him with good precision. She crouched back down behind a wall, but there was no time, someone was already at her location and stabbed her in the stomach, she fell to the ground, but before she lost consciousness she saw a man get behind the man who stabbed her and stabbed him in the heart.

"Quincy….." That is the last thing she said when she lost consciousness.

Quincy couldn't believe what just happened. The same girl from the bar, she looked so familiar.

"Quincy who is she huh? Do you know her?"

"I only met her tonight Dante. She looks really bad though. She looks like someone gave her quite a fight. I say we take her to Roman's house."

"Ok, and I am only saying ok, because she saved our asses." Dante said laughing. Quincy picked her up in his arms. As he carried her to her car and put her in the back seat gently. Quincy stopped and moved a piece of hair behind her ear. He noticed a necklace that she had on. It looked like the same one he gave Serena. He got that thought out of his mind, for some reason he was seeing Serena in his thoughts more lately. He had to get her out of his mind, she is gone. If she is gone why is it so hard to get her out of his mind.

CHAPTER 17

Jude woke up, she sat up holding her head, her head still hurt. She then remembered what had happened. She had saved Holly. She hoped Holly got to Kieren and Trista. Then she had helped those two vampires kill those hunters. The vampire hunters. One of them got to her and stabbed her where she had already been stabbed and then she got knocked out. She stood up. She was feeling better. She looked around the room, her guitar is gone. She walked to the door and found it was unlocked. She walked down the hallway and wondered around the house, careful that she didn't run into anyone. She would get her guitar later. She had to get out and make sure Holly was ok, make sure no one had followed her or would come for her. She tried to find a phone, and found a door, when she opened it, she found a phone at the desk. She went in and went to it.

"So, you are finally awake?" Jude turned to find a man sitting in a chair by the fire putting down the book he was reading on the table next to him. He had dark brown eyes and garnet colored eyes. He had a young appearance, yet his eyes said he had lived a long life. He dressed formally in his white blazer, black shirt, red tie, white pants, and black shoes. Even though he wasn't smiling he had this calm stoic look. Very elegant yet authoritative. Yet, she couldn't help but feel warmth and gentleness from him as well.

"You were hurt pretty badly. You were knocked out for three days."

"Who are you?"

"You must not be from around here or recognize me. Understandable I don't get around much. I like my privacy. But you have heard of me."

"Well, like I have heard of you, you most likely have heard of me."

"I have, seeing you in that outfit, you are the boogieman for vampires." Jude laughed

"Boogieman, that is what I am being called. Just great, So you have heard of me, who are you."

"I am Roman Pierce."

"The king. I thought you would be bigger."

"Haha, I thought you would be a guy. I guess we all can't get what we want now can we?"

"You know I have never met anyone more wittier than me."

"I have, my wife. She has enough wit for the both of us I am afraid."

"Why did you bring me here and where is my guitar."

"Straight to business it is then Jude."

"Definitely."

"I got a message that you were sent to kill me."

"Ah. From who. No let me guess, Umm, a man named Klaus, or Zero."

"Are they right?"

"Do you think I would stupidly try to save your people if it were?"

"I don't know, but Zero is here now. Asking to take you with him."

"That was fast."

"Should I bring him in?"

"Can I make a call first. Prisoners always deserve that one call don't they?"

"I will be here while you make it."

"Fine." Jude picked up the phone calling Trista.

"Hello."

"Is she there?"

"Safe and sound, sleeping right now. Haven't heard from you in three days. Need us to go in?"

"No, I am good. I am guessing you know what is happening?"

"Savitar, said he was your guardian. He is not your guardian for nothing."

"So you can come in when you are ready?"

"Yes."

"Hold on." Serena put the phone down on the desk. "Roman, Where is Zero?"

"Near the front entrance."

"You can go. I will contact you when I can." Jude hung up.

"I am gong to see Zero alone."

"Why would I let you do that?"

"To prove a point. If I am lying you can kill me. I am not going back to Zero."

"You have an hour. You will be escorted by two of my friends. Quincy and Sebastian."

"Splendid, but they stay far enough away. Still in ear shot but away. There are some things I don't want to get out."

"They still are in ear shot of the conversation. Fine."

Jude opened the door to find Quincy and a man standing next to him. That must be Sebastian she thought.

"Are you ready?"

"Yeah." As they were walking Jude noticed that Quincy still didn't know who she was, she didn't want to reveal her true self but soon everyone would know who she was.

"Is Quincy telling me the truth, that you shot an arrow at a vampire hunter?"

"It is whatever."

"Whatever seriously. I have always wanted to meet the boogieman for criminals for the vampire world. Even the hunters have heard you. Is it true that you died once?"

"If I died I wouldn't be here."

"Where did you get that necklace?" Quincy asked seriousness in his voice.

"Jude stopped and turned to look at them both before she entered the study to face Zero.

"Look, I am just a halfling who can fight that is it. I got this necklace as a gift. I just want to deal with this so I can leave I don't belong here. So if you will excuse me." Jude entered the study and closed the door behind her. She wasn't ready for Quincy to find out who she was, if he didn't notice who she was, why should she care anything about it, but deep down inside she did.

"Why are you here?"

"Is that anyway to greet the man who is going to save you?"

"Save me, you want to make my life a living hell."

"There is that. I thought you would be happy to see me."

"Not so much, Zero. You sent me after innocent people and expected me to kill them.

"Tsk Tsk Serena. I am surprised Roman let you out. I just want you to come home so we can help you. Your father is so worried about you."

"Screw you, you bastard." Zero Laughed.

"It is just so hard to keep a straight face pretending I care about your well being. Oh and about your comment, we already did that, and we can do it whenever I want to. Remember that." Zero said smiling looking Jude up and down.

"You asshole, telling the king of all people I was trying to kill him. You could have found another way to get to me."

"Who the hell cares how I got to you. I told you I could find you. You really ruined everything you know by killing Catherine."

"You two sent me after an innocent family."

"An innocent family who is dead. You were too late to save them. You just had to be a savior didn't you? As for Catherine she was a means to an end, I was surprised that her kid didn't kill her along with his father. They were both pathetic."

"Oh, you don't know, I saved the girl. I got to Catherine first before she could get rid of her."

"You bitch, do you know what you did?"

"Saved an innocent yes I do." Zero punched her which made her get pushed back, and held her against the bookshelf by her throat.

"I can get rid of you anytime I want, do you hear me. I own your ass." Zero kissed her roughly on the lips and let her go. And straightened his suit. Jude wiped the blood from her lip.

"That is a cute little outfit you have. I can't wait for you to beg me to get you out of it." Someone kicked through the door and kicked Zero to the ground.

CHAPTER 18

Quincy left while Sebastian guarded the door. He didn't feel like guarding the door. He stopped before he opened the door. Ever since he saw her he had been curious about her, he dropped his hand and flashed back to in front of the door of the study.

"Quincy, you got to really listen to this, this Jude girl is telling the truth, one thing I don't think her name is Jude." Sebastian whispered.

'Go get Roman and everyone I will listen in." After Sebastian left Quincy went closer to the door. When he heard the guy call her Serena, he couldn't breathe. Especially when he talked about his mother and father that girl was Serena. He should of saw it when she told her that quote on her arm. Only Serena ever told him that one night after he helped her recover from her father hitting her. He is the only one who told her he would love her infinity times infinity when he was telling her how much he cared for her. Serena was alive he couldn't believe it. Quincy heard a slam against the book shelf and that man's voice. Quincy couldn't control himself, he was too angry and excited from Serena being back, and this man harming her. He kicked the door open and kicked the man down to the ground and punched him, and stood back up. He turned to stare at her. He had no words.

"I....Why..." There was the girl he thought was dead for years, it would seem for all her wit she was also at a loss of words.

Jude couldn't believe what Quincy had done, she was speechless. When he stood up and looked directly at her she was speechless. She couldn't say a word. She looked away and noticed Zero stood up. Roman came through the door with Sebastian and a woman, and two other guys Serena hadn't met yet.

"What the hell is going on here?" Roman said calmly.

"Well, this man attacked me for no reason. He deserves some kind of punishment. I was just talking to her to see reason." Quincy walked forward to attack him again but Sebastian held him back.

"Down wild cat."

"Sebastian let me go." Quincy said in a cold angry voice.

"Everyone relax!!" The woman said.

"Thank you my sweet Lizzy. I just got a call. Jude I am sorry to have misjudged you. Zero you lied, I have it in my right mind to kill you. But because of the call I leave it up to Jude to see what to do with you."

"Screw you, you don't scare me and neither does that whore."

"You and I have unfinished business, Zero. You deserve what I am going to give you."

"And what is that?"

"Death."

"Oh really."

"Can I have my guitar case back please."

"It is behind that desk." Jude went behind the desk and found the guitar and opened it and got two swords out of it. One she bought for herself and one given to her as a present from Savitar. She threw it to Zero who caught it instantly.

"You really think you can beat me?"

"Well, we will know soon won't we?" Jude and Zero faced each other for a long while, swords at the ready, one waiting for the other to make the first move. Zero traced to right in front of her, Jude blocked fast, and jumped back, Zero came at her fast, she kept blocking and backing up. Jude traced behind Zero, but he traced and swung his sword behind her, she didn't have time to block and got hit on the back. He was going to swing again but she backed up. Jude charged at him, traced behind him and gave him a cut on his back before he could get away. He turned and backed away. "Look who is weak now."

"Still you, you bitch." The battle went on like this for the next few hours, Jude getting a hit here and Zero getting a few hits until they were both back to staring at each other, both tired.

"You are done."

"It is not like you are all full of energy right now."

"Ready?"

"Lets end this already." Jude and Zero both ran toward each other and swung their swords at each other. As they ran past each other. They both were still for a while.

"I guess I will see you in hell, I will save you a seat." Zero said smiling. Zero went down to his knees and fell down on the floor and disappeared. Jude sheathed her sword and picked up her other one off the floor and sheathed that one as well and put them back in her guitar case and closed it. She faced everyone in the room.

"This is why I like fighting non humans they disappear afterwards, easy clean up, except this is why I hate fighting in the house, we still have extra clean up." The girl named Lizzy said. Jude picked up her guitar case.

"Thank you, for letting me finish what I needed to do. I have to go." Jude said this while not looking at Quincy.

"Wait, I hear you are a Harrison."

"So, you are a Pierce, what game are we playing?"

"I like her, can we keep her?" Dante said laughing. Ignoring him Roman continued.

"You know you were meant to be part of the society right?"

"I am not part of the society. I am girl you know."

"I am aware, but someone looked into your family. Apparently your parents knew and never told you. But you were the first girl born to be in the society. The first halfling too."

"it doesn't matter if I am destined for it or not. I don't care. I am leaving anyway."

"Why?"

"Look you all seem nice, whatever, but I am best alone, always have been."

"How about a week."

"What?"

"A week, stay in New Orleans and stay at our home for a week, it is not like you have any other place to stay. Then at the end of the week if you don't like us then you can go."

"What makes you think I would want to stay."

"You would want to stay because you find family here. Also Savitar wanted me to tell you to stay for a week or he is going to take that guitar of yours and kidnap it until you stay in one place. Just to let you know he already took it."

"What… he was never fair. Fine, one week, I am here."

"Excellent, boys why don't you introduce yourselves."

Dante walked up to her and shook her hand. He was an interesting character to her. He had black spiky hair with brown eyes. He had three piercings above his left eye and silver earrings on his ears. He looked more like a bad boy type. He was wearing a black t-shirt and blue jeans, with red and black tennis shoes.

"Welcome Jude or is it Serena, I can't decide which to call you, they are both good names for you. You fight good by the way, I can see why they call you the boogieman."

"You ask a lot of questions. Thanks. Um, no one has called me Serena in a long time, only Klaus, Haley, and Zero called me Serena, everyone else called me Jude. I would rather everyone call me Jude."

"Jude it is then." Another man stepped up. He had mahogany hair, with lightly tented blue eyes. He was a man that possessed immense beauty that looking at him made her blush. He looked noble. He was wearing a buttoned down black shirt, blue jeans, and black shoes.

"Nice to me you, Jude, my name is Alexander. Nice of you to join us." He smiled at her.

"Um, nice to meet you too." Serena looked away blushing.

Another man walked up to her, he had a bored attitude. He had a muscular build, he had short brown hair, and brown eyes, he had one silver earring in the middle of his left ear. His white shirt was unbuttoned and he was wearing black jeans with black and white converse. He had a tattoo in the shape of a flame on his right arm.

"You can really fight, welcome to the team."

"I am not part of the team yet."

"Oh you will, Roman never gets the no, he always gets the yes.

"Is that so?"

"Haha yeah. My name is Cole."

"Good to meet you Cole." Lizzy stepped forward to introduce herself. She looked beautiful with long dark black hair, with dark eyes with a little purple to them. She was wearing a white blouse, with a red skirt and red heels.

"Hey, so my full name is Elizabeth but people just call me Lizzy."

"Good to meet you Lizzy. Sorry about the mess, I will clean it up since it was my fault."

"Don't worry about it, I was just joking, we can clean it up later. Between you and me you actually did me a favor, I wanted to remodel this room anyway. You just won me an argument." Lizzy said smiling.

"I can hear you, you know. You can stop gloating now." Everyone laughed. Jude noticed that Quincy was gone, he was nowhere to be seen. "I guess he didn't want to talk to me." She whispered silently to herself.

"Jude, Jude." Jude got out of her thoughts and looked at Roman who had been calling her.

"Did you hear me?"

"No, I am sorry, what did you say?"

"I said you can stay in the room that you were resting in. Your belongings are already there."

"How did….Never mind. Savitar is going to pay for this."

"Haha, he knows your moves before you even make them I wouldn't bother with it."

"How do you know him?"

"Savitar and I go way back, he got me out of a pretty bad situation, lets just say I owe him one, and he owes me two. I lost track a long time ago."

"If you guys don't mind I wanted to go back to the room and rest for a bit."

"That is fine. No worries, we can talk more tomorrow."

"Ok. See you guys later."

CHAPTER 19

Quincy couldn't talk to her, he didn't know what to say. Now she was talking about leaving again. He couldn't face her. Not now. Quincy heard a knock on his door. When he went to open it he was hoping it was Serena, but it was Roman who appeared.

"What is it Roman?"

"You left pretty quickly down there."

"I wasn't in the greeting mood."

"Aw why, because you met the boogieman, were you that scared?" Roman said with a smile.

'I am not in the mood Roman. Just leave it be."

"You need to talk to her."

"What?"

"Do you even know what she has been through?"

"She is the one who pretended to be dead all these years and didn't let me in on the secret!! I have been mourning a girl that never died!!"

"Everybody has a reason for something. She had a reason for throwing away her old life for this one."

"I don't care."

"You do. Savitar told me the whole story and brought me up to speed. The man you met was Serena's guardian.

There is a reason Savitar does everything. Serena told him that night she didn't want anyone to know, he respected her wishes but with you he didn't. He sought you out that night letting you know in his own way what had happened. He told her in a couple of years she would see you again."

"What, why would he tell her that?"

"Savitar is a lot of things, I will never understand it, but he took her under his wing. He treats her like the daughter he never had. He wants her happy. He knows that you made her happy. He noticed it the first time he talked to you face to face. So it would be cruel to not go talk to her now."

"What do I say?"

"Anything, just talk to her. I have a feeling she wanted to talk to you before you went to your room to sulk." Roman left the room. Quincy didn't know what he was going to say or what was going to happen, but he wanted to talk to Serena and see what happened.

Jude was getting changed, she was putting on her t-shirt after putting on bandages on her arm and on her cheek, and leg, and back from her fight with Zero. She couldn't believe one of her nightmares were gone. Just two more to go and she could sleep peacefully at night. Jude heard a knock on the door. She walked up to it, her knife in hand and opened it ready to fight. She paused as she saw Quincy at the door.

"Don't stab me, I am not here to fight."

"Sorry, habit. What do you want?"

"You always answer your door half naked?"

"I am used to being alone. What is it?"

"Could I come in? If you open the door wider I brought some tea, you still love tea right?" Jude opened the door wider and walked away from the door to sit at a table as Quincy came in.

"No offense, but I can't drink that." Quincy went to sit across from her at the small table and put the two mugs on the table in front of them.

"Why is that?" Jude didn't say anything, she just ignoring him. Quincy watched her waiting to say something anything to end the silence.

"Why?"

"Why what? Oh, why didn't I keep in touch?"

"Where were you all this time?"

"I can't…I"

"There is a reason you still talked to me three days ago. Why you kissed me. You can tell me. I just need to know, because I don't understand how you could have gone all these years and not even let me know you were alive. How you could let me go on knowing that you were dead that my family had killed you. I killed them for you."

"That was you, Savitar didn't tell me that. How did you find out they had me?"

"Savitar, told me to go to the bar you always went to, I went and found that my brother was gloating about it just like Savitar said, and the rest you know or heard. He just didn't tell me you were alive."

"He was respecting my wishes without respecting them. He found a loophole. He is good."

"Well, he did say we would meet again right?"

"How did you…."

"Savitar told Roman, who told me."

"Why didn't you kill me back then, that is what I never understood especially when your father told me. I wasn't going to believe it until I heard it from you. You had every opportunity to do it."

"I couldn't. I kept looking at this beautiful girl, who held more than just my curiosity but also held my heart. I wanted to take away her sadness and pain. I wanted to tell you that weekend. I even told my parents that I didn't want to do it. I gave up fighting for hire for you. I wanted to be a better man for you. When I thought you had died, I kept thinking I didn't protect you, I didn't get to you in time. I kept seeing you in everything I did, even when I kissed you I always suspected it was you. Serena where have you been?"

"That night, I really thought I was dead. I didn't want anything to do with my old life, and I vowed to get revenge on everyone who had a hand in what they did to me. Savitar taught me how to fight, and after a couple of years after that night, I had finally went back and my father knew I was alive. I had hurt a guard at some point for recognizing me. He sold me to Zero, and after a month I met him and…" Quincy went to stand and put his hand on her shoulder, she got up and pushed him away.

"Please don't do that. I don't like to be touched much."

"Why?"

"Anyway, I met Trista and Kieren you would like them they are nice, they taught me a lot, like playing the guitar and taught me how to use weapons, and other stuff, we became friends. I stayed there for six years, and then I used that time to become a killer for hire for Klaus and Haley. Zero called Klaus, he wanted me to kill two humans because they saw him and your mom together selling humans and tasting them. I said I wouldn't do it, Catherine killed one of them I rescued one from her and killed her. And after that I helped you and Dante, with those vampire hunters and here I am. You know the rest."

"You went through a lot. You never answered my question you know."

"About what?"

"Why don't you want to be touched, you avoided the question. Also why you don't drink what a person made themselves?"

"Just leave it alone ok."

"What did they do to you?"

"What?"

"Zero, or my father, my mother, i don't know who, what the hell happened?" Jude stayed silent. "Serena tell me, please." Quincy was getting closer to her until she was backed against the wall.

"Please don't…"

"You always could talk to me, you can talk to me now I am the same person. I won't hurt you. I promise."

"What do you want me to say huh. I got tortured by your family, and even worse than torture once in a while by your brother and his asshole friends, who touched me. Savitar got me out of there, where my only father found me half dead twice in his life. When I came back to Klaus I had found out I was sold to Zero, where he… well, stupid me I tried to trust someone, he cooked me dinner, I drank the wine that he made, since he helped me recover and helped me when my own father dropped me in the woods. He mixed something in his made drink for me. And took advantage. I lost six weeks, woke up on and off and apparently I kept telling him and everyone he brought in to take me anyway they could have me that I was good. Apparently in my drugged induced state I liked it. I lost days and weeks and a month. Happy. Are you happy that you know everything. Huh. I became this way because of everything that has happened. I stopped caring, until I had those two fucking targets, and I saw you again. I was fine the way I was. I didn't want to go back to you because I didn't want to go back to my old life I wanted a change. I didn't want to be the weak girl anymore." Serena stopped talking with tears streaming down her face, she went to the bed and sat down. Quincy was speechless, he wished he was the one who killed Zero, he wished he could have taken everything that had happened to her away. He wanted to protect her.

"Serena, I am sorry, I wish I could have been there to protect you."

"You don't know how many nights I wish you were there. When I kissed you, it all just came back to me." Quincy walked up to her.

"Everything?"

"It is nothing ok." Quincy walked up to her and went down on one knee.

"Do you remember what I told you?"

"What are you talking about?"

"How I could be your protector."

"I told you then and reminding you again, I don't need a protector."

"If you get hurt like you did tonight, then I need to show those guys and anyone who messes with you why they shouldn't."

"Ha, why shouldn't they hm, when they think I deserve it."

"Because you are mine my graceful goddess, and I take care of what is mine." Jude smiled.

"You are so sure I am yours huh. How do you know that."

"I was drawn to you since the first time I saw you dance, before I even talked to you I was drawn to this beautiful witty girl." Quincy moved his hand and touched her cheek.

"Quincy we shouldn't do this."

"I am just checking your injuries. Your cheek is fine. I am just feeling you for more injuries. Your legs are fine. I want to make sure you are healed."

"I am, so you can go now." He smiled, and the look was pure devil.

"Healed for what I want to do."

"You don't have to look or keep touching me while you do."

"Doctor's orders." His devilish gleam intensified in his darkened eyes.

"Liar, you didn't take me to a doctor."

"What is this?" Quincy lifted up her t-shirt over her head, he focused on her nudity, an appreciative gleam in his eyes, her skin was very flushed.

"What is what?"

"This on your stomach. There are a few scars over it, but I can still make it out. Is that your family's crest?"

"Yeah, I believe it is."

"Why did you brand it here?"

"What makes you think I had a choice in the matter?" Quincy was angry when she said that. They must have held her down he thought. He wanted to kill her father for what he had done to her. He pushed her down onto the mattress.

Straddling her legs with his and leaned against her. Jude couldn't fight the attraction she had for him even if she wanted to.

"Quincy, what we had was just a passing thing that is it. It was only a fling. We shouldn't do this. I am a danger to everyone I get into contact with." Quincy kissed her forehead waiting and watching, to see if she was going to pull away.

"I told you then I always laugh at danger. Come back to me my graceful goddess. You know you dreamed of us together again like this. Just the two of us alone. Cuddled up while I kept you safe from any harm."

"I did not dream of you. I dreamt of a god coming to me every night."

"Haha, a god huh?" He said with a wicked smile,

"He was incredibly handsome."

"You were dreaming of me and I know it." He took off his shirt and threw it to the floor. She looked at his chest, the same bronzed skin that always took her breath away every night since she met him, even in her dreams. She wanted to reach out and touch him, to feel his skin sizzling beneath her fingertips.

"Why didn't you tell me you were alive?"

"I just, I wanted a new beginning. I wanted to forget everything that ever happened. Not about us. You were the one person that I could let in, but after I found out what I did, I didn't trust anyone anymore. I kept being put in one hell into another. It took me a long time for me to be strong again. The only thing that had me going all this time was knowing that one day I was going to see you again. When Savitar told me you were just gone, my heart stopped yet he said I would see you again. It kind of hurt you know that you didn't recognize me."

"Trust me Every time I saw you, I kept thinking that is Serena, I just couldn't believe it since I thought you were dead. You even had the locket I gave you."

"I couldn't get rid of it. It is the only thing I had to remember you by." He pulled her into his embrace. "Serena, you were mine since I first saw you. I knew it, you were my beautiful witty graceful little dancer." Quincy moved a piece of hair behind her ear. She pressed her lips against his, giving herself willingly to him and was immediately transported to before everything bad happened the past few years.

"Are really sure you want to be with a girl like me, there is no going back."

"I don't want anyone else but you. Infinity times infinity remember. You are mine, I will always protect what is mine." He looked in her eyes for any doubt. When he didn't see any he kissed her greedily and possessively. No more gentleness. And she loved it. His hands tangled in her long hair, and he grabbed handfuls, his gaze was looking over her nakedness. She couldn't take her eyes off his face, the chiseled features, the predatory look. She had wanted to be in his embrace for so long, dreamed about the day when they would be back together. This dream would be short lived. Soon she would be going after her father and mother. The last fight she expected to get through. She didn't know if she would survive. If she had to pick how she would spend the last few hours of her life this would be it. With the first man she would ever love now and forever."

CHAPTER 20

Four Nights later

"What are we doing here?" Cole asked in a bored voice.

"Sere...I mean Jude wanted to talk to all of us together. So Jude, you have the floor."

"So it would seem that you just always work and have no play."

"It is fun killing vampire hunters, does that count at all?" Sebastian said with a smile.

Well, moving on. One night of fun, I have a couple of nights to decide to see if I want to stay, and I don't want to use them working. So I suggest we go to my friend's club and relax."

"You know that actually sounds like fun. I think we could use a night out." Dante said smiling.

"You just want to get girls, that is all you are worried about." Cole said with a bored tone.

"Well that too." Dante said laughing.

"I don't care what we do, whatever will be fine with me." Alexander said.

"Roman I think that is a great idea, we haven't been out and about in a long time. We are long due for some down time. Come on, we can take one night off of work." Lizzy said.

"Well I don't want to go against my wife now do I."

"Since when?"

"Haha, well not all the time my dear Lizzy. You are on Jude. Hey Quincy you never said if you wanted to go."

"What ever Serena wants to do, I will gladly follow her."

"Isn't that so sweet, looks like Quincy has a girlfriend." Sebastian said smiling.

"Quincy loves Jude, Quincy loves Jude, Quincy loves Jude." They all chanted.

"Ok Ok, whatever. I can kick all of your asses if you don't stop." Quincy said smiling.

"You can try." Jude just laughed. She wanted this one last moment with them. These past nights with them were fun even if she didn't know them for long. She needed to meet up with Damien to find out where her parents were. They had moved from their place in Long Island ever since they heard that she had killed Zero. Tonight was the night that she would get her revenge.

When they got to the club they got in and sat down near the bar.

"I have to admit this bar isn't as lame as I thought it was going to be Jude." Cole said with a smile.

"See, told you so."

"Hey, dude, so this is the new guard detail of yours you have been hiding from us. Finally glad to have you back in the world." Kieren came up and stopped in front of her.

"Ha ha, Kieren is most likely happy that I haven't been around because I am not here to beat him in kicking his ass."

"Ha ha, very funny, you are worse than Trista one day that bragging will get you in trouble. I can beat you anytime." Jude and Kieren laughed.

"Kieren, meet Dante, Lizzy, Cole, Sebastian, Roman, Alexander, and Quincy."

"The infamous Quincy, I have heard a lot about you. Well, as her best friend…"

"Second best, as her first best friend, if you ever hurt her I can hunt you down and literally hurt you."

"Trista I presume."

"Yeah I am." Trista said with a smile.

"Jude please, state to my dear loving wife that I am your first best friend."

"Sorry dude, I have to side with Trist on this one, I mean she is the one who taught me the secret in order to get passed you so…"

"Oh whatever, I see how it is. Quincy no matter what, I am number one. Don't mind them." They all laughed.

"It is nice to meet all of you though."

"It is nice to meet you guys too. You have a nice club here." Quincy said.

"Thanks, it took a long time to create, but we did it."

"How is Holly doing?"

"Adjusting pretty good in New York. Liking that she has an apartment to herself. She wants you to come visit. She also said to tell you thank you for saving her." Jude smiled.

"I will visit her soon."

"Can I get anyone drinks?"

"scotch for me." Cole said

"Beer for me and Lizzy please."

"I am going to scout out the crowd for a bit." Dante said smoothly. Sebastian laughed.

"I will have a beer waiting for you when you get shot down enough times.

"Quincy? What is your poison?"

"Scotch."

"Good man.Jude, what about you?" Jude wasn't paying attention she saw Damien sitting at a table near the stage.

"Jude, Jude!!"

"What, why are you screaming?"

"I asked if you wanted a drink?"

"Oh no, I am fine."

"Serena, honey, are you ok?" Quincy asked with concern in his voice.

"I am fine. On second though I will be right back you guys, I see an old friend, and if I remember correctly he is not great with crowds. I will be back."

"Ok." Jude kissed Quincy on the cheek and went to see Damien.

"Hello Damien." Damien looked up from his conversation with a woman to see Jude standing there.

"It is time for you to go."

"Aww, are you really sure you want me to go baby?"

"If I said it I meant it. Good Bye." The woman got up, and showed off some of her cleavage while doing it.

"You don't know what you are missing." She walked off while Jude took the seat that the woman had sat in.

"So, what can I do for my dear old Serena, that you had to interrupt me trying to get laid?"

"Where are they?"

"You don't call, or write, or anything it is just straight to business with you."

"Just tell me where they are."

"Why, it looks like you have a good thing going so far. You even found Quincy, I never thought that would happen."

"I have unfinished business with them, you and I both know that, now where are they."

"Look, even if I knew where they were, you are literally out numbered. You have forty or fifty guards at the most on the first floor, you have your mother, sorry Haley to deal with, she is tough, but then you have your father too. I know you are good but not that good."

"I took out Zero."

"I am sorry, but Zero is a weakling. Ok not that weak, but you go in by yourself and you will get destroyed. Plus you have two guards out front to circle around the premises."

"Don't care."

"They are at Catherine's house that she had here. I know, shocking isn't it. I told them it was a bold move even for them, knowing that you were so close, but you know Klaus, he says you wouldn't dare come to them."

"Then come with me and help."

"Ha ha, funny. No thanks."

"After the hell you helped put me through you owe me a big favor."

"Low blow, I tried to help."

"And turned right around and helped those assholes."

"Fine you are right, I will help you earn your long awaited revenge. But you know that you might not make it back right. With just the two of us."

"I am aware. I have made piece with it."

"Fine you go ahead steak the place out I will be right there."

"I will wait twenty minutes, if you are not there I am going in without you."

"Twenty minutes fine." Jude left out the back.

Damien pulled out his phone to call Savitar.

"What Damien."

"Nice to hear from you too. Serena is on the move. I thought you should know."

"Well a little injured at the moment."

"You, injured from what."

"Got ambushed, I am still game for a fight."

"What do you want me to do, she asked me to help."

"Interesting, I guess she guilt tripped you into that one."

"You are correct, but I still would have helped either way."

"Go help, I will be there in a few, I am going to get some more help."

"Ok. See you there then."

CHAPTER 21

"Roman you want to dance" Lizzy asked excitedly.

"How can I say no to you." Roman's phone started ringing he noticed that it was Savitar calling. "One second Liz. Savitar, what can I do for you? If you are checking on Jude again she is adjusting well, I have a feeling she is going to join us."

"You lost her."

"What do you mean?"

"She is going to try to get her revenge in a bit, I have to talk fast."

"Wait, what do you mean she is getting revenge, she doesn't even know where Klaus is."

"An old friend told her and she is out for blood. You need to get there, I will give you the address, but some of your men have to go and help her otherwise I don't know if she will survive. I am going and our mutual friend Damien is helping, but just three is not going to do it."

"I will send some, but I have a feeling that they would all want to go." Roman hung up. "Sorry Lizzy, have to take a rain check."

"What's wrong sweetie. Talk to me."

"Looks like we have to work after all. Guys come here." Everyone gathered around Roman.

"You know Roman you could have added a please to that."

"No time. Quincy, bad news. I think Jude just used us to get here."

"What are you talking about?"

"Nothing. A couple of us have to work tonight. Jude is getting her revenge tonight, and apparently she is up against more than she can chew. So who is going?"

"We all are."

"I thought you would say that. I hate that I have to stay behind, but…"

"Don't worry bossman, you are the king after all. Plus you have a wife now."

"We will go." Kieren said from behind them.

"Excellent, I get to see both your skills, Jude keeps talking about it."

"Let us hurry up shall we, my girl is waiting."

"We will get to her Quincy I promise, you won't loose her again." Trista said reassuringly.

"I hope not."

Jude was in the guard booth. She had just killed one of two of the guards, when someone talked to her through the intercom.

"Hey kid, I am surprised of you."

"Seriously, how do you always know where I am?"

"I have friends in high places. Anyway we can talk all we want unless you would rather…"

"Rather what? Sav, hello."

"Do it in person." Jude turned around to see Savitar outside the booth smiling. She walked out to confront him.

"What are you doing here, and what about the other guard?"

"Don't worry, already taken out at your command my sweet knight."

"Damien called you didn't he?"

"Well, you can't just go up against sixty guards."

"Damien said forty or fifty."

"Well, I just scanned everywhere. So it is sixty."

"I can take them."

"Hold it, you can't go in there guns blazing you need help."

"I am fine on my own I always am."

"You were never alone you know."

"I was."

"I was always right there with you Serena. There to protect you and I am protecting you now. Just wait for a second."

"I know, but you don't need to protect me anymore. I can do this."

"Just do an old vampire like me a favor and wait."

"Wait for what."

"I believe he is waiting for the calvary to get to you in time before you sneak in there." Jude turned around and saw Quincy and the others including Damien with Trista and Kieren.

"You didn't think it would be that easy to sneak off did you, well if you don't know how wrong it is to sneak off on your own party then that is just wrong. I mean I get it is your party you can cry if you want to, but not leave." Kieren said.

"Guys, and girl, I know you know by now, because of Damien the little snitch…"

"Hey, they didn't know because of me they just followed me."

"Whatever, but, whatever he told you, or Savitar, I am fine with going in alone. This is my family, my revenge, my problem."

"Don't you get it at all?"

"What are you talking about Quincy?" Quincy walked up to her and put his hand gently on her cheek, making sure he looked her in the eyes.

"You are our family. Especially mine. I will not loose you again, not to Klaus. We will stay out of the way when you decide his sentence, but you can't stop us from killing those guards who try to come at you."

"Why would you do this for me Quincy?"

"I love you, you crazy girl, get that through your head. You have people who care."

"Thank you. All of you."

"Now that we got that out the way lets kill some guards."

"Serena while we are dealing with the guards you can go ahead up. We will all cover you."

"Wait, Sav, what about your injury?"

"What injury?"

"I got stabbed a bit no big deal."

"Who did it?"

"Your mother snuck up on me. Just stab her back for me I will be fine kid."

"Quincy, look after Savitar for me."

"I will."

"Wait, seriously, I am fine." Jude lightly hit his side. Which made Saviar grunt a bit."

"My guy is taking care of my guardian."

"Fine."

"Fine. We have our plan, thank you all of you. I know for the vampire society we just met, but I am glad we did, you guys are like my brothers I never had. Trist, you are my dance, and singing partner, and my best friend."

"Number one right?"

"Haha, you have competition which is a tie. You are like my sister, I have always wanted. Kieren, you are my best friend and the first person I could be fun with. The first person who could make me laugh since everything that happened. My first actual friend. Sav, you have always been there for me, you and Damien even if he is a snitch. Sav, you have protected me and made sure I was happy even if I wasn't, you got me here to New Orleans. As far as I am concerned you are my father. Quincy, you, my first love and last, the first person I told everything too and the first person to accept me throughout everything, I love you. All of you, no matter what happens I am glad I knew each and every one of you and I am happy to fight by your side."

"Lets go kick some asses." Sebastian said smiling.

"I will see you guys in there." Jude said while walking to the front door. When Jude opened the door there was a guard at the base of the stairs.

"Hey, who are you?"

"I am here to see Klaus and Haley. They were expecting me."

"No we weren't." Klaus was walking down the steps. Looking smug as usual.

"So, you found us. Who told?"

"Does it matter? I am here to finish what I started."

"Really, you really think you can beat me. A pathetic weak girl like you?"

"I know you hear about me, I am not that weak girl anymore that I once was. I owe you for all the scars you have given me."

"I dare you to try to get to the top." Jude started walking forward.

"GUARDS!!! You didn't really think it would be that easy to get to me did you?"

"You know for a second there, yeah, I kind of did." Jude said with a small smile. "But hey, you have your army, I brought mine." Jude pulled out her phone and pressed the send button. Savitar and Quincy were at the front line of her friends who all came in to be by her side.

"Savitar, Damien, you betray me like this?"

"Well, we never really were on your side, we were on hers, every step of the way. So you see, we never could have betrayed you it is that simple." Savitar said with a smile.

"You, I know you."

"You knew my father, Nick, I killed him, just like Serena is going to kill you."

"Isn't this so sweet, the two lovers found each other again. I hope you are enjoying the whore. I hear she begs for it." Quincy stepped forward to finish him but Jude held him back.

"He is mine."

"As long as I get the leftovers. Cut him somewhere special for me." Quincy kissed her on the cheek.

"Definitely."

"You have to get pass them first. Guards, kill the bitch." The guards rushed toward them as they all stood back to back in a circle.

"Serena go ahead, we will hold these losers off." Jude dodged a sword, then took her knife out and stabbed him in the chest.

"Sweetheart, go, and be careful."

"I will. I l…" Quincy kissed her.

"Save it for when we see each other again my dear." Jude dodged some guards and killed a couple until she finally reached the top of the stairs.

CHAPTER 22

Haley was gathering as much money as she could. Jude was here and coming after her and Klaus, she needed to get out of here as fast as she could. When she was done putting the money in the bag, she walked over to the door and opened it, when all of a sudden she was kicked in the stomach forcing her backwards into the room on the floor. She looked up to see Jude in front of her. She got up and tried to kick Jude back, but missed. Jude tried to punch her but Haley kept blocking. Haley kicked Jude in the face and knocked her down to the floor. Haley was getting her sword and the bag of money and was about to leave when she saw Jude standing at the door with her sword in her hand.

"Savitar gave you that old sword of his did he?"

"Of course he did."

"Haley."

"Serena."

"I alway wondered, what did you do or say to Sav, to make him snatch out the heart of your friend?"

"Hm, I tried to have him killed for stabbing me in the stomach during one of our sessions."

"Bad Idea."

"You know what I did, I tried to have him killed again. I managed to get him in the side, but that bastard is good at evading I can give him that."

"He told me to get you back for that."

"I will make you suffer until your last breath." Jude ran up to Haley and tried to swing her sword at Haley's throat, but Haley blocked it with her sword. They were in that position for a while. Jude looked down at Haley's chest then looked back up at her eyes. Jude moved the swords out of the way then took out Haley's Heart. Haley disappeared.

"Looks like you are the one suffering." Jude said smiling. Jude walked out of the room and was in front of the door where Klaus should be in. This was it she thought, the final fight. She opened the door to find Klaus sitting at his desk.

"I am surprised you got this far. You surprised me at every turn."

"You know how I love to be unpredictable." Jude went to sit down on the couch in the study room, while Klaus was at his desk.

"I have a couple of things to talk about with you, before our showdown comes to an end. When it comes to you, and any subject that includes me and anything I am related with, you lie, or wit your way out of it. I am going to ask some questions and I want you to answer them."

"Fine, what do you want to know?"

"You know, you always talked about saying you wanted out of this world of mine that I created, when you loved every second of it."

"I hardly enjoyed it."

"You enjoyed killing every one of them in order to get to me didn't you."

"Yes, I did, but it was all to get away from you. The same people who ruined my life all those years ago. The people down stairs were the ones who were really the ones that were there for me no matter what."

"Hm, I am such the bad guy of your story. Why did you want to get away from me so much, when all I ever tried to teach you was to be the lady you are today, independent, when you have always been nothing but weak."

"The thing is, you taught me nothing. The only thing you wanted me to be is your obedient little puppet, you never wanted a daughter. From you, I learned to trust no one, to always look over my shoulder. The only person who taught me to trust again is Savitar, he is the only father I will have. The only family I have are the ones who are fighting your guards right now. My family never sold me, or tortured me. When I count the many things you could do to me, you handing me to someone to be tortured and raped to teach me a lesson would be last on my list. Could you do what you did, of course you could, but I never expected that you would or could do that to me. Your own daughter."

"Then you underestimated me."

"You and I have unfinished business." Serena stood up with her sword in hand.

"You aren't kidding." Klaus said with a smile. Klaus transported to her and tried to cut her, but she quickly saw the move coming and jumped back in time. She charged with a thrust to his stomach, but he jumped back. He transported to her again and knocked the sword out of her hand. He was about to stab her when she took her sheath and Klaus put his sword in that. Serena moved his hand out of the way and took her hand and put it through Klaus's chest.

"Interesting, you had a heart after all." Klaus coughed up blood.

"Savitar taught you this huh when he doesn't even care about anyone."

"Of course he did, he was the only father who protected me all these years." Klaus coughed again.

"Well I will see you in hell then Serena." Serena took the heart out of Klaus's body while he was falling his body disappeared along with his heart. Serena couldn't believe it was finally over. Serena took one last look around the room. She was finally free to do whatever she wanted, no longer did she has to look over her shoulder. She picked up her sword and sheathed it. She took a match and lit it and threw it to the ground. She walked down the hall and went to the steps to find only Quincy there waiting for her.

"I figured I could rescue the girl this time. I sent everyone home." Quincy said smiling.

"Good thing, the house is burning anyway, we have to go." Quincy transported to right in front of her and brought her towards him.

"Well then, lets go home, there is still the matter of you deciding if you are staying or going." They transported out of there and into a future that Serena was still unclear of.

CHAPTER 23

A few nights later

Serena left Quincy in his room to sleep. She had gotten a beer from the refrigerator and went back to the first room she was brought in when she was first introduced to the society. It was only a few hours until she made a decision. After everything that happened she was finally free to do whatever she pleased. Learning that she was always destined to be apart of the society one day, she always did the opposite of what she was meant to do. There was a knock on her door. she put on a pair of shorts and a black t-shirt, and black heels. She walked up to the door and there was no one around. She looked up and down the long hallway. No one was there to be found. Serena was about to close the door when she looked down and saw a small light blue box with a white bow on it. She also saw a white card next to it. She picked up both the box and the white card. On the card the only two words that were written on there in cursive were the words surprise and welcome. She opened the blue box and saw a beautiful sapphire ring, one of her favorite colors. She wondered who had left her this ring and note. When she turned around, from behind a bag went over her head. she tried to struggle but someone was there holding her tight so she couldn't struggle. She didn't know what was going on. She stopped struggling. Whoever these people are, she was going to wait and see what they wanted. Whenever she had the chance she would attack whoever had the audacity to try to sneak up on her. The person who held her made her walk until they were outside. They were getting in some kind of vehicle. Serena sat there still as stone, she could tell she was in the French Quarter by now, hearing muffled voices of tourist walking around going to the different restaurants or clubs. Suddenly they stopped, she heard multiple people going out of the vehicle and closing the door which meant there was a group of people who captured her. They took her inside, she didn't know where they were, but hopefully there were no witness's around for what she would do to her abductors. Suddenly the person holding her let her go and walked away from her. Then someone took her hand and put something on her finger. The person backed away from her. When no one else approached her, she heard a familiar voice.

"You can take that bag off your head." the man said. It couldn't be she thought. She took the bag off her head and saw Roman, Quincy, Dante, Sebastian, Cole, and Alexander surrounding her all showing no emotions on their faces looking calm. She looked around and noticed that they were in the club that Kieren and Trista owned.

"What the hell are we doing here, and what is with the cloak and dagger. I seriously want to rethink staying with you guys."

"We all went through it Jude, even the king of vampires did." Alexander said.

135

"Went through what? Doesn't matter I am going now, if this is a cult kind of thing you have the wrong girl. You shouldn't have snuck up on me either, very few people can. You all got lucky."

"Jude, relax, whatever you decide to do we have to do this, well we want to do this." Cole said in a serious tone.

"Do what? What are you guys talking about?"

"We want to initiate you in the society. You are going to be officially apart of it. Apart of the good fight against the vampire hunters."

"I haven't made a decision. Is this to pressure me Roman because I am damn well not going to succumb to peer pressure."

"Haha, nothing like that, we all talked about it, and no matter what, we want you to be apart of this society I recreated. Not just because you were meant to be apart of it like the rest of us, but in this short time you have become our friend and our family. We want you to know whether you stay with us or you leave us, you will always have a place to call your home. You will never be alone, you will have a family." Serena was speechless, she never really knew what the true word of family meant, not until she met these vampires.

"Thank you, for letting me in your family."

"The ring we gave you symbolizes that you are part of the society. we each have one. All a different color." They all gathered close to her.

"Jude, being a part of the society doesn't mean just guarding me, you will be apart of a family. Your problems are our problems. We will always be there for you and vice versa. We are your family no matter what happens." Roman walked up to her.

"Give me your hand." Serena gave Roman her hand and made a cut on her palm.

"Squeeze your hand and spill a few drops of your blood into this cup" All the others did the same thing.

"After you drink our blood combined we will all be family." Serena drank the blood out of the cup. After she did they all cheered.

"I can't believe you all did this, literally I was planning on hurting you guys if you guys turned out to be strangers."

"You should have been there when we initiated Cole. He struggled so much he actually punched Alexander. We had to knock him out." Dante said laughing.

"It was a bad time, I had just gotten out of something drastic and also I said I hate when people sneak up on me. I warned all of you."

"I am the one who got to knock him out so I felt a bit better afterwards." Alexander said. Everyone laughed. They all got back in the car and drove to Roman's house. When they got back there Serena opened the door to find Lizzy, Kieren, Trista, and Savitar there to greet them.

"Surprise!!"

"I am surprised Damien isn't here."

"He went off to finish some things I will fill you in later." Savitar said walking up to her.

"I am also surprised that they actually got you here."

"And miss the chance to see you being initiated, not a chance." Savitar said smiling. Serena looked around at her friends she didn't want to leave any of them behind, especially Quincy. She loved him. He had been quiet since they got back, even when they were in the club. She loved

Quincy so much, but she had to go. No one will ever be safe with her in their lives.

"I have something to say. I am very happy to have so many people in my life, no matter how they came to be in it. You all have helped me through so much…" Serena paused and she wiped a tear that was coming down she looked at Quincy and no one else. "Umm, but I have to go. I have no other choice. You mean so much to me this isn't about you. I just can't…." Tears started falling down Serena's face and she went back to her old room to pack with Quincy right behind her.

"Serena, why are you."

"Quincy just please go."

"No, I won't let you get away from me, not again. Serena I love you so much, don't leave."

"I have to, don't you see, I just hurt everyone I come into contact with. I am always alone and better off for it."

"You were never alone, those people are right there beside you I am right here at your side."

"Quincy don't. This is hard enough."

"Then don't do this, you know I care Serena."

"Do you know I hear things, the months before my parents were killed I got around. Secretly before that guard found me. and then after that, after I got away from Zero. I heard a lot and I found out some things."

"What are you talking about?"

"I know you were having me followed."

"What, how do you…"

"Well, I was walking in my favorite bar, something was off about Rebbecca. That was the first time I saw her in months. The last thing I remember is she wanted nothing to do with me as much as she has tried to help me in the past and said I was her friend. I cornered her, she was watching me too carefully. She told me you knew I was alive. Which made me wonder how you knew, no one knew. I came here not knowing what to say to you, and I didn't want to bring it up so I pretended nothing else was wrong."

"Serena, I…Fine, I knew. I went back to New York to get a few things. I thought I had saw you at one point walking around. I thought I imagined it but something told me to follow my gut. So I did. I saw that you turned around and I knew at that moment it was you. I couldn't believe it, and I couldn't face you, so I tracked down your friend and paid her to follow you. She never told me about the danger you faced."

"But you knew I was alive and never came for me. You lied to me."

"Serena I….I didn't know what to say."

"Well, here is what I am going to say get out. I am leaving tonight. Until you can find the right words I am leaving."

"Serena…." He didn't have a chance to finish the sentence she was gone. Serena reappeared in Savitar's apartment in Long Island. She was crying, she couldn't believe she just did that she thought, but it had to be done. She was better off alone. Someone passed her a beer, Serena looked up to find Savitar.

"I think I need something much stronger than that Sav."

"I would just stick to the beer if I were you kid."

"Why do people lie?"

139

"Well, to shield people from the truth I think, otherwise everyone would go around miserable knowing every single detail that people try to hide."

"You make no sense."

"Yeah I know, but there is a reason for everything, and if you have to lie to protect someone I am all for it. If it is worth lying about."

"Quincy just…"

"I know."

"You knew."

"I know a lot of things. Especially things that happen with you kid."

"Why didn't you say anything."

"Eh, I bet he had his reasons."

"He said he didn't know what he was going to say to me. He never even came for me or tried to help me."

"He would have if he could."

"How do you know."

"That boy loves you kid, this isn't just about him, I know having not to look over your shoulder is weird. I also know that you haven't had luck in the friend department. But Serena, everyone who was at that house loves you and would kill anyone for you. Quincy would die for you. And me, lets just say I have more cause to kill anyone who harms the girl who is like a daughter to me. I have seen you grow up and struggle, and become strong when you had to be. I saw how bit by bit, every one of your friends put back the pieces of your heart."

"Sav, I can't go back I just can't."

"You can. You have to trust them. You are not alone anymore. We are all right here with you. Even Quincy."

"I have to go back. Don't I?"

"You do kid. You know I will always look out for you, but it is not just me anymore. You don't have to be scared." Savitar hugged Serena and stepped back. Serena waited for a moment, she didn't know what to do. No, she knew, she had to go back. She transported back to Roman's house. When she got there she was outside and it was raining. She walked back and forth deciding what to say. She walked through the front door. She didn't know where everyone was, she heard music coming from the study. She went through the door and heard Sebastian talking. He paused while looking at her, everyone turned to see what he was looking at and saw her. Roman turned the music down.

"Serena, this is a surprise."

"I am sorry, I have something else to say."

"Serena you are shivering do you want a jacket or get some clean dry clothes…."

"Quincy I am fine. I have to admit, I was scared. All my life I have been alone and I was used to that, that was my comforting place. Everyone I came into contact with me always betrayed me somehow, but then I meet all of you, and everything changes. You guys and girls, were there for me when no one else was. You guys are the first family that I have ever had and I want to stay if the offer still stands."

"Well, it is pass the time that you were supposed to tell us, but we accept, welcome to our family Jude." Roman said with a smile. Everyone cheered and turned up the music and started partying

"Serena, you all can call me Serena."

"Good, because I got tired of making the mistake and calling you Serena, then calling you Jude." Cole said laughing.

"Can you turn down the music." Quincy said to Roman. Roman turned down the music as Quincy walked up to Serena.

"Serena, I am sorry that I wasn't there to help you once, and I promise to never again let you down. I should have told you I knew you were alive, I just couldn't find the words, but here they are. I love so much, I was scared to approach you because I thought you were going to disappear, but I never wanted to hurt you. I promise I will always tell you everything, I will always protect you…"

"Quincy it is ok I was just scared so…."

"No, I have to finish. I will always be on your side and at your side whenever you need me." Quincy got down on one knee.

"I already asked Savitar for his permission, otherwise he would have destroyed me. Serena, will you marry."

Serena looked up from Quincy and saw every one of her friends, and Savitar awaiting her answer. She was so lucky to have found friends like these. She looked back down at Quincy, she was also lucky to find true love with this man in front of her.

"Yes, I will." Quincy got up and put a ring on her finger. And lifted her up and twirled her around while he kissed her. She was finally surrounded by friends and family who truly cared for her and she would never be alone again.

KISS OF THORNS

PROLOGUE

Cheryl Hughes stated that "The truly scary thing about undiscovered lies is that they have a greater capacity to diminish us than exposed ones. They erode our strength, our self-esteem, our very foundation."

Serena was standing on the deck of a boat that had white lights on the rails and flower petals everywhere around her in her white wedding dress drinking champagne, she was looking out in the water, she turned around bringing the champagne glass down to her side and saw a gun pointed at her and had a sad worried look on her face.

"I am so sorry." The moment she said that the gun went off twice and hit her in the abdomen she got pushed back and fell over the railing into the cold water it took only a few seconds as she closed her eyes.

CHAPTER 1

Few weeks Earlier

Serena opened her eyes slowly she heard the shower running in the bathroom then turn off. A man came in wearing just a towel and walked up to her in the bed and kissed her on the lips."

"Morning sweetie."

"Morning." Serena said unenthusiastically, she got up slowly and walked to get some underclothes out of the dresser and went to the bathroom to get ready for the day.

"Are you ok, it seems like you are really out of it."

"I am ok, just not looking forward to tonight, nervous really. It is a big party, and if the mixer doesn't go well, well I am pretty much not going to get a good job as a party planner after that."

"It will go fine my dear, I will be there to calm you down."

"Thank you Sebastian, but you don't need to, I have Cassie with me as well, so you can go ahead and just mingle with the guest of the party."

"I will be there for you anyway to make sure you are still sane at midnight." Serena kissed him on the cheek. "Aren't you so sweet my dear Sebastian."

"Are you going to see Cassie now?"

"Yeah, I just have to shower and get dressed and I am meeting her at the owner's backyard to see if everything is prepped and ready to go for tonight."

"Ok, I will see you tonight then."

"Ok, see you tonight."

"No, No, put the roses on that last table to your right. Put them in the center. Perfect guys."

Serena walked into the owner's house, she hadn't met the owner, but he must have a lot of money to buy this house. A pool on the outside, a theater room downstairs, a fantastic kitchen, a baby grand piano, a dining room, a gym, maybe she would get a house like this one day. It really was a great place. Serena walked through the kitchen in order to get to the backdoor to get to the backyard. Everything was looking good so far, the food was looking good in the kitchen and tables were getting prepped to put the food on. The fire and ice party was perfect so far. White and red table cloths, roses on every table, A fire is going to burn in the middle, candles on every table, the servers in white suites with red ties, there is no reason to think something will go wrong. Serena walked over to Cassie to see how she was doing.

"Serena finally, I am going nuts."

"Hello to you too my dear best friend"

"I am sorry." Cassie hugged her and stepped back. "I am just freaking out because this needs to go well because if it does, we will get a lot of offers to do other parties from the people coming."

"It is ok, Cassie, just breathe, everything looks fantastic. What about drinks?"

"In the kitchen we have water, Sangria, ice bowl, made with a fruit blend with rum, citrus rum, and blue orange liquor, and the Fire bowl, made with pear, peach, and orange vodka with orange liquor and cranberry juice. Already made, and a bartender to give out different kind of liquors for people who don't want mixed drinks. We also have white wine and red wine out. Blue teal Moscato and Plum Loco wine. All put out in Glasses, and the drinks are made and ready to serve."

"Good" Where are we food wise?"

"Food is all cooked and ready to serve. If more people come, then the cooks are ready to cook more, and for desert Strawberry Siam parfait."

"Fantastic, see everything is ready to go Cassie. Oh what about our dresses."

"They are both upstairs. For me a strapless white short mini dress with silver beading and for you a sexy red strapless floor length chiffon evening dress with ruffles and a split that comes up to your thigh, the perfect dress for you."

"Aw, you know me well."

"Of course I do, hence me being your best friend. We are allowed to change in the guest room."

"Ok, have you seen the owner yet?"

"No, but he sent an email saying he loved what he was seeing, I don't know how he sees anything if he hasn't come by his house. Serena said. "Maybe we will see him tonight."

"Is Sebastian coming tonight?"

"Of course, white tux with a red tie. He is coming to make sure I relax tonight, but Cassie, can you keep an eye on him and make sure he mingles with people, so he doesn't have to keep tabs on me all night."

"Of course I can."

"Shit, look at the time, it is almost 6, the party starts at 6:30, we have to get ready and into our dresses."

"The party will go really well." Cassie said.

"I hope so Cassie."

Serena noticed through the window that guest started to arrive, now the party was beginning, the music playing people laughing and talking amongst themselves, the servers serving drinks, and people getting to their tables. The party is going well, she saw Sebastian looking as handsome as ever arriving and taking a seat at the first table. The party is beginning, time to go down there and manage it.

Serena walked downstairs to the kitchen, and into the backyard. Everyone was in there seats or walking around. People enjoying the food. A server passed by and she took a glass of wine. She went over to the table that Sebastian went to.

"Looks like the party is a success my dear."

"Thank you Sebastian, Cassie and I tried our best. How do you like everything so far?"

"Everything is fantastic, the food, the drinks, everything."

"I am happy you like everything. I need to go around and make sure everything is going ok, plus find the owner of this house and see how he is enjoying the party. The weird part is I have never seen him and he wasn't even part of setting the party up. Are you going to be ok?"

"Yeah, go work sweetie, I will go mingle."

"Ok, I will find you later Sebastian."

CHAPTER 2

Cassie, knew she should be looking over the party instead she was in the bed with her friend upstairs. She knew that she should help Serena, but she hadn't seen him in so long, he was traveling watching as people adored his photography and bought it. He always didn't want to show up at anything he was hosting or anything for him he would rather sneak in. He walked out of the shower dressed up to go to the party.

"Shouldn't you be getting dressed Cass?"

"I hardly get to see you and you just came back for the party, come back to bed."

"You know I can't, I want to see how people are enjoying the party, it is the least I can do for not getting involved in your work. I always hate planning parties. Besides, don't you have to help your friend with it to make sure everything is going ok?"

"I guess."

"When am I going to meet your friends anyways, it has been a year already."

"I just want to keep you to myself you know. Plus, I don't like her that much anyways. She took something from me. I am planning something big for her."

"Aw, still playing the games I see."

"Like you aren't, I know what you did with that one artist."

"She was over charging for one of her paintings she deserved it." Charlie said smiling. Cassie went to get dressed and kissed Charlie on the cheek. Cassie didn't want Charlie to meet her friend yet, he was the ace to put her big plan in motion.

Serena was walking around making sure that everyone was enjoying themselves, so far she and Cassie had so many offers tonight to plan other parties, and one wedding reception. Finally she saw Cassie at the party, she was talking to Sebastian, she wondered where she was most of the night, but she would ask her later. Tonight was a good night, except it was already nine at night and she has not seen the owner or at least heard he was here. She went over to a server and got another glass of wine and went into the house and went to the living room where the piano was, she needed a break from the party. She put the wine on a nearby table and started playing the moonlight sonata. When she was done playing the song she heard slow clapping and she turned to see a man leaning on the wall. She looked him up and down and saw that he was the most handsome guy she had ever seen. She looked back up to his face before he noticed that she was truly looking at him.

"That was a great performance miss."

"Guest aren't allowed in the house without the owner's consent."

"My apologies, I just needed to get away from the party. What about you, are you not a guest?"

I am the party planner, I just needed a break from it all. Also it is ok, it is not like the stupid owner is here anyway."

"Great party, it looks amazing, and everything was delicious including the drinks, and I don't usually like mixed drinks. So this owner, you have something against him?"

"Oh yeah, that jerk hasn't even been apart of the party planning, so me and my partner were alone in this fantastic house to do whatever we wanted, granted we are good people so we didn't take anything and I made sure no one did, but we could have, I have never seen him. Plus on top of that, everyone is out there in there beautiful attire and the party is going on and the owner has not shown up, I mean he could at least say good job. Not that I am a woman that needs praise or anything I just, he hasn't been apart of it and I did this alone, I love to see the look on people's faces when they see the decorations and how everything looks. I love making magical nights or magical days for people, everyone deserves that at least once in their lives. But no, not even that, so I am playing the piano, and drinking wine, and taking a break from the party. Anyways, what about you, why aren't you enjoying the party with your friends?"

"Well, before I get to that, you did a great job tonight. Sorry I was a stupid jerk who didn't help with the party and didn't...well I did at least show up." The man said with a smile.

"Oh, man, you're the owner. Wow, I am embarrassed, I am so very sorry sir." The owner sat down next to her on the piano bench.

"Don't worry about it, I was a jerk as you called me for not checking in with you. You see, I hate planning parties, my friend told me to plan the party as a way to celebrate, but I think it was an excuse to get together and get drunk. I almost didn't show up."

"Why wouldn't you want to come to your party?"

"Just because I am just used to it. I take pictures for a living I have people wanting my stuff, people putting it up in galleries, I was actually in Paris, and someone had put some of my pictures in their gallery and I watched as a potential buyer. I just hate, to be myself around people, to be judged, do they like the party do they absolutely hate it. I don't appear so people can talk about me all they want, I just like to hear it like I am everyone else. To stay in the dark, and I will know what people truly think of me, than me being around them and telling me what I want to hear."

"I know it is hard to trust people, but you know, you can trust me, to tell you the truth, I know that I am a stranger you just met, but I will tell you the truth. I try to tell people the truth anyway, and I don't like keeping secrets never could."

"Well thank you, this all started a year ago anyway, me pretending to be someone else at my own revealings or parties. Anyways, so you won't call me a stupid jerk again, my name is Charlie."

"I am so sorry Charlie for saying that, I always say what is on my mind and mixed with alcohol I definitely get straight forward to the truth. Oh, my name is Serena."

"It is ok Serena, it is refreshing to hear someone speak their mind about me. My friends know I am here so they make sure that they speak their minds as much as possible."

"I am always here to help I guess. Do you play or is this just for show?"

Charlie chuckled and he put his fingers on the keys and started playing fur elise. Serena smiled, after he was done she slow clapped for him.

"I guess the piano is not for show after all. You play very well."

"I have been playing since I was six I believe. What about you?"

Since I was ten, I love trying new things. You are not as boring as I thought you would be."

Charlie chuckled, "You thought I was boring huh?"

"Well since I never met you, I thought you were just this rich guy who just liked parties and nothing else, you were just this boring rich guy who liked to throw his money around." Serena and Charlie both laughed.

"And now, what do you think?" Serena looked into his eyes then and then to his lips and back to his eyes, his lips tempted her to kiss them, but she knew she shouldn't because she had a fiancee.

"You are just full of surprises and just a big mystery. Since you love a good disguise"

"You are the one who is the mystery, that I would love to solve." They were looking into each others eyes, Serena could feel a connection between them like it was fate that they had met, but she had to get these thoughts out of her head, she shouldn't be having these feelings for another man. They were interrupted by Sebastian.

"There you are, I was looking for you, we should be leaving now."

"Sebastian, I am sorry, I lost track of time here. This is Charlie, he is the owner of this house."

"Hi, we really should be going Serena, it is late."

"Sebastian, don't be rude, plus I can't go yet, I have to help with clean up, and help everyone pack up. It is my job."

"It is not your job, you did your job now, it is midnight and I want to go. Cassie is leaving now."

"Well why don't you give Cassie a ride home, hmm. I will meet you at the apartment later."

"How are you getting home then, I am not driving all the way back to the Hamptons from the City."

"I will drive her home." They both looked at Charlie.

"Yeah, Charlie will drive me home."

"Fine, Charlie can drive you home, he better just do that and nothing else."

"Sebastian, don't be rude." Sebastian was already walking away.

"I am so sorry about Sebastian, it has been a long day for him. I am just really sorry for his rudeness."

"It is ok, don't worry about it."

"It is not ok, he always does this, every time he has a bad day he is rude to everyone, I always try to get him to relax, but he hardly ever does. I am sorry, to tell you this it is not your problem. I am going to go clean up now. It was nice to finally meet you."

"I will help you clean up and then I will drive you back to your apartment into the city."

"Thanks, I appreciate it."

"Well you threw me a party so it is the least I could do for you."

Serena and Charlie finished cleaning up and Serena got into Charlie's car and he was driving her home.

"Thanks for driving me home Charlie, you really don't have to do this."

"Oh, don't worry about it, it is my pleasure, especially when you threw a party for me."

"What made you get into photography?"

"I guess it is a little like why you like party planning. I love to capture those magical real moments in life. Not the fake moments when people dress up and pretend. A picture can never tell a lie, you can dress it up as a lie, but looking at it you see a person's true self."

"I guess that is why you like to pretend you are someone else huh."

"I guess so, just to get the truth out of people. Well, here you go, home sweet home."

"Thanks again, I really appreciate it."

"No problem, oh, before I forget I will send you the last check in the morning."

"Thanks, have a good night Charlie."

"You too Serena."

As he saw Serena walk up those steps and enter the door to get to her apartment, he didn't want to let her go, he wanted to go after her, but he knew he shouldn't, she had a boyfriend, that never stopped him before. Maybe I am just tired he thought. He got that thought out of his head. It is not like he would ever see her again he thought to himself. He drove off.

CHAPTER 3

As Serena opened the door, she called out for Sebastian, but he wasn't in the apartment. The way he wanted to get me home, it seemed like he wanted to talk in private she thought. He was so rude tonight and she didn't understand why. She tried to get that out of her head, he did have a long day, but she was going to talk to him about it tomorrow. She went to get ready for bed, and then her thoughts went to Charlie and how she wanted to kiss those lips tonight. Charlie wasn't anything she expected him to be he was more down to earth and more like her than she thought anyone could be. She got that thought out of her mind, she shouldn't be thinking about another man since she is going to be married soon. She went to get into bed. It is not like I am going to see him again anyway, she thought to herself.

Serena woke up to see the spot next to her was still empty. She couldn't understand why Sebastian did not come home last night. She got out of bed and took a shower and when she got out Sebastian was sitting at the desk.

"Sebastian, you got home rather late, and by late I mean very late. Where were you?"

"I was drinking late last night, I took a taxi and accidentally went to Cassie's apartment instead of ours, she let me stay the night. She didn't call you?"

"No, she didn't, at least I know where you were. I am glad you are alright. Now, can we talk about last night, because someone was a little rude to the owner who is paying my checks. What was up with you last night?"

"I am sorry I was rude with the owner ok, I had a bad day, had a lot of drinks, they collided hence the rudeness, I am sorry sweetie."

"It is ok, are you feeling better?"

"Yeah, I just hated loosing my case, I am feeling better, just waiting to hear on another case." Serena walked up to him and sat on his lap and kissed him on the lips.

"You will win the next one sweets, definitely." There was a knock on the door, Serena went to open it and found Cassie standing outside her door.

"Oh, hey Serena, I thought you were opening the store today."

"I thought you were......well I will get dressed and head down there to open it. Come in. Are you coming with me after I get ready or, what are you going to do? Because all we are doing is getting ready for my wedding, we have no clients for a while."

"I need to run some errands first and then I will be there."

"Ok, take your time, I just have the reception to go over. Oh, by the way, thanks for taking care of this goof, while he was out drinking."

"huh, oh, no problem, it was my pleasure." Serena was dressed and ready to go.

"Are you coming Cassie?"

"I will go in a second I need to talk to Sebastian about something."

"Ok, I will see you both later then." Serena said while walking out the door.

After Serena closed the door, Cassie walked up to Sebastian and sat on his lap and pulled out a cell phone.

"So, you left your phone at my place last night, I just wanted to come and give it to you, I didn't expect for Serena to be here though. Good thinking telling her that I just helped you out she fell for it."

"We have to be more careful if we are going to keep doing this Cassie my dear."

"But it is much more fun when we almost get caught."

"Cassie, Serena can't know about this, you get that right, just because we had sex last night doesn't mean I am breaking it off with her, it meant nothing between us, it was just because I was upset got me."

"I got you, but what does twice mean?" Cassie got up and slipped out of her dress, and Sebastian got up from his chair and walked toward her he was inches away from her and stared into her eyes, "I will let you know." He kissed her on the lips passionately.

Serena finally arrived at her party shop, she went in the back to drop off stuff at her desk and went back to the front to work on her reception, and to work the register and watch for people coming in to buy party decorations or to plan a party. While she was working on her wedding she heard the bell on the door to let her know that someone had walked in but she didn't look up.

"Knock knock, didn't think I would see you here. I didn't even know you worked in here."

She looked up and saw a man looking as good as he did last night with his brown eyes and short brown hair, he was wearing a black leather jacket with a white t-shirt, blue jeans, and black boots. He also had a helmet with him, if he drove a motorcycle she definitely couldn't get him out of her mind then she always had a thing for guys who drove motorcycles. Charlie was the one man she didn't expect to see again, the man that was on her mind since the party.

CHAPTER 4

Charlie went back to the city the next morning. He wanted to talk to Cassie about a new game, since he was bored. He wouldn't be traveling for a while because he needed to start working on pictures and he had gotten a job to take pictures of the Smith wedding that was taking place in 4 weeks from today. He was going to ask her last night, but she never came back to his house. So he went to get a new camera for the wedding, and he was going to stop by her party shop before he went back to the house. When he finally got to the party shop he walked in and expected to see Cassie at the register, but when he opened the door and walked in he stopped, he saw a brunet haired girl working at the register, she looked up for a moment and he saw that she had chocolate brown eyes that he had been thinking about since he dropped her off last night at her apartment. Serena was so beautiful with her long flowing hair in a ponytail even though it looked so much better down, and she had on blue skinny jeans with black and white chucks, and a white lace crop top, while wearing a black leather jacket. He had to admit the girl knew how to draw attention and knew how to dress. Just then he wanted to go up and just kiss her right there but he knew he couldn't she was seeing someone, nothing could ever happen no matter how much he wanted it too. She was busy doing something so she didn't notice that he had come in.

"Knock knock, didn't think I would see you here. I didn't even know you worked in here."

"Ch…Charlie, hey, I didn't expect to see you again."

"Oh so it is a bad thing huh?"

"No, it is not, it is good to see you again, I just wasn't expecting it. What are you doing here?"

"Well I thought someone worked here, but I guess I was wrong, I found you instead."

"Is that a bad thing, I feel like a second choice for prom."

Charlie laughed. "It is nothing like that, She just told me she worked here, I guess I misunderstood. Sorry, I guess it is my turn to have that embarrassing moment, it is not like it is good to see you too, I will just shut up now."

Serena chuckled. "I was joking it is ok, who are you looking for, maybe I know her."

"Cassie Blake."

"Ah, you know Cassie, she is my best friend, and told me this morning that she had some errands to do, and will be by later, knowing Cassie, and since we don't have clients right now, she either won't come today or she will be in later this afternoon." Serena said chuckling.

"That would be her" Charlie said laughing.

"How do you know her?"

"She is one of the friends I told you about, I just wanted to talk to her about something, but it can wait, I can just call her later."

"Oh ok, I didn't know you two were friends. I guess that's why she wanted the party to be perfect. It all make sense."

"Yeah, so what are you looking at anyway, when I came in you were really into it."

"A wedding, actually, mine and Sebastian's, I was working on the reception, and the wedding is in 4 weeks from today, and Sebastian is not helping one bit, so I am mostly doing this alone, and sometimes with Cassie, but apparently not today. But soon I will be Mrs. Sebastian Smith."

"Smith?" Charlie said looking shocked.

"Yeah. I think it is more better to take the guy's last name, if I just kept my last name it will feel like the wedding wasn't official."

"Is your wedding reception on a boat?"

"Yeah, how did you know?"

"That was your husband, I didn't put two and two together until now. I am sorry I am rambling now. I got a call from my friend who sells my pictures and artwork, he got me a job here, and he said it was to take pictures of a wedding, last name Smith, I was suppose to meet the couple tomorrow."

"You're the photographer, wow, this is a very big—

"Coincidence yeah."

"I guess we were meant to meet after all like—

"Destiny, just like I was thinking."

Serena moved a piece of hair behind her ears and looked up into Charlie's eyes, there was something about him that attracted her to him. She couldn't say what it was, but she couldn't help but think about what it would be like to be with him and to feel his lips on hers to feel him touch her she stopped thinking about it, she was getting married in 4 weeks, she should be thinking about Sebastian and her life with him.

"Well, um, I guess I will see you tomorrow then, I will tell Cassie you dropped by."

"Um, would you like to grab dinner with me?"

"Wh…What, dinner?"

"Yeah, you know, strictly professional, to talk about the photos and how you want them done and everything."

"Um, yeah, people have to eat right, I mean you eat dinner, I eat dinner, everyone eats dinner. Um, sorry, I am rambling." Serena said smiling awkwardly.

"What time are you leaving here, I can pick you up here."

I get off at 6. Let me give you my number."

"Ok, I will see you then."

"See you then." Serena said as he walked out the door. I am in trouble, Serena thought to herself, No I am not in trouble, this is strictly professional, nothing to worry about.

Cassie was about to walk into the party shop when she saw Charlie talking to Serena, she opened the door slowly so the bell wouldn't ring to hear some of thier conversation. She went back outside and started walking back out to her car. She knew how to get to Serena and ruin her. Her plan will start now and it was the best plan ever.

Sebastian heard a knock on the door and opened it, it was Cassie, Cassie walked right into the apartment without a word.

"Cassie, come right in." Sebastian said sarcastically.

"Sebastian, I am sorry to barge in like this, were you busy."

"Just reading up on a case, what's up, come to have more fun?" Sebastian said with a smile

"No, I have come for a different reason. You see I have my suspicions that Serena is not being honest with you."

"What do you mean?"

"I think she has a guy on the side. I think his name is Charlie, she met him at the party last night."

"The owner, I will confront her about it."

"I wouldn't. Sebastian, I have a proposition for you, I don't think you should refuse."

"Well Cassie, tell me all about it."

CHAPTER 5

Charlie opened the door and went into the living room only to find Cassie there.

"Cassie to what do I owe the pleasure of your company?"

"Oh, this is business. I want to play a game. I know you love a good game."

"I do especially yours."

"Well there is this couple who is getting married in 4 weeks, and I want the guy."

"And what, you want me to break it up?"

"Yes, I want you to seduce the girl into falling for you so I can tell her husband she is a cheating whore and call off the wedding." Cassie smiled.

"What did she ever do to you."

I tried everything to get him to notice me."

"And he fell for her, aww so sad. Who is the target?"

"Sebastian Smith and Serena Bennet."

"I am suppose to be their photographer, I met Serena. As much as I love a good game, I don't want to do it."

"Why not, she deserves it."

"It is too easy."

"Lets make a wager then, I bet you couldn't do it."

"You know I like a challenge. What do you get if you win?"

"I get your house."

"And if I win?"

"I will give you me. The one thing you have been obsessing about since we started this on and off thing."

You've got yourself a deal honey."

"Happy hunting Charlie." Cassie said as Charlie was going to his room.

Let the games begin Cassie thought as she walked out of the house.

Serena, was waiting outside for Charlie. She really wasn't ready for this date, no, not a date, professional dinner. Hopefully he saw it that way. Of course he did, there is no way he was into her, but the way he was staring at her today it seemed he wanted to be more than just friends. She got that out of her head as she saw him pulling up on his motorcycle. "You are not going to make this easy for me are you." She said to herself aloud. Charlie got off his bike and took off his helmet.

"Hey, are you ready for dinner?"

"Yeah, where are we going?"

"Well it is only a few blocks away, we can walk, but we are going to Bubba Gumps. Is that ok."

"Yeah, I love that place."

They finally got to the restaurant and took a seat in a secluded booth.

"So, what would you like me to take pictures of at the wedding reception?"

"Mostly any of the happy moments, of course when people give their toasts, um, when we all sit down at the table, the father and bride dance, and any other happy moment at the wedding, oh and also when Sebastian and I cut the cake."

"That is fine, I can do that."

"And we will pay you tomorrow for it."

"That is cool. Why don't we take a break from work for a second, work is all I ever talk weeks about."

"That is fine. You know meeting you and looking you up, you don't seem like the mysterious brooding type."

"What makes you say that?"

"People have said you are outgoing and it seems like you get along very well."

"Well, only for my friends I am outgoing for other people not so much. I just don't like people seeing the real me you know. Like I said before that is why I like being mysterious."

"You know what your problem is you take yourself way too seriously, and you use sarcasm to cover it."

"I do not."

"Yes you do. You should try to lighten up."

"I am lightened can you drop it please?"

"Fine, ok." They sat there in silence until Serena made funny faces at him.

"What are you doing?" She made another face."

"Sop it, it is distracting." Charlie said smiling.

"It is ok, you can relax, I won't tell anyone." Serena said smiling.

Serena looked back down at her food, while Charlie just looked at her amazed.

When they finished dinner they walked back to the shop.

"Thanks for inviting me to dinner."

"Thanks for the company." Charlie kissed her cheek and then her other cheek, then slowly he moved to kiss her lips. He has wanted this ever since he first saw her.

Serena's heart skipped a beat as Charlie kissed her cheek, and then her other cheek. Her heart slowed as he kissed her on the lips the one thing she kept thinking of. The kiss felt so good. She put that feeling aside and pushed him away.

"Charlie, I am getting married I can't. I will see you in 2 weeks with the payment ok instead of tomorrow. Bye."

As she was leaving he wanted to pull her back and kiss her again, but he should't he kept reminding himself that this was a game and nothing more.

Cassie was hiding in the restaurant and followed Charlie and Serena back to the store, and saw the kiss and took a photo of it. This would come in handy in the future she thought. She then sent it to Sebastian's phone.

When Serena got home she undressed, she couldn't stop thinking about the kiss she had shared with Charlie, it was hot and passionate, nothing compared to what she felt with Sebastian. Being with Charlie just felt so right, he really understood her. Sebastian was being standoffish as we got closer to the wedding. She got this out of her mind she was getting married in 4 weeks, nothing not even Charlie was going to stop it. She can't start having doubts now.

CHAPTER 6

Sebastian was sitting at the bar having a drink before he went home. He couldn't believe that in 4 weeks he was going to be married to Serena. Marrying Serena was right, being with Cassie was just a one time thing even if he was with her twice. He has always loved them both, he lost his chance with Cassie, but now he had a chance with Serena. Time will only tell who he chooses, but he didn't have to make that choice now. He felt a vibration from his phone, he looked at it was from Cassie, she wanted him tonight no doubt. He looked at it and saw a picture of Serena and the owner of that house Charlie kissing and it had read, "I thought you should know." He couldn't believe it, Serena wasn't the girl he thought she was. Cassie was right after all. If she wanted to have fun then so could he. She was going to pay for this he thought. He chugged the last bit of scotch from his glass and went to see Cassie. He couldn't believe he almost was sorry for having sex with Cassie.

Charlie heard the door bell ring and he opened the door to find Serena standing there breathing hard.

"Serena what are you— He couldn't finish the sentence because she kissed him passionately, and he kissed back. he pulled her in and closed the door and pushed her up against it. They stopped kissing enough for Serena to take off his shirt and unbuckling his belt. he stopped and looked at her. Suddenly he felt wrong, he didn't know what he was feeling. This would win him the bet, he would win the game, but it didn't feel like a game, not anymore.

"Serena I am sorry, I can't. You have to go." Serena looked surprised and left in a rush.

What was he thinking, he shouldn't have let her go.

What was she thinking, she shouldn't have done that, she was getting married soon. It was good that he stopped it before it got too far. Then why did she feel so sad and angry over that, that she had no answer for.

CHAPTER 7

Two weeks later

"Morning" Charlie woke up to see Cassie on top of him.

"How did it go with Serena?"

"If you are asking if I had sex with her the answer is no."

"She shot you down because of her stupid morals."

"No just the opposite."

"what went wrong?"

"I don't know, she was in front of me and ready to do it, but I was...I just didn't feel right about it."

"Your telling me you had a chance to fuck her and you didn't, you are a chump."

Charlie pushed her off of him. "You better go, she is coming here today to give me the check."

"Oh she is not, I am giving you the check, it seems she doesn't want to see you and she didn't tell me why." Cassie said with a smile. But it seems she is setting up for the wedding anyway on the boat.

Charlie arrived on the boat looking for Serena and he finally saw her in one of the rooms. She was trying to make it perfect for her and Sebastian he knocked on the door. Serena turned and saw Charlie, she was not ready to face him after what happened two weeks ago, she never thought she would see him until the wedding. Charlie walked into the room and closed and locked the door. He went up to her and was inches away from her.

"I am sorry Serena."

"I am impressed you showing up here."

"I think that I…" They both looked each other in the eyes, Serena was drawn to him and Charlie was drawn to Serena. He kissed her and she kissed him back.

"Are you sure about this Serena?" Charlie asked.

"Yeah." They started kissing again. Not knowing who was behind the door Cassie was listening to every word with a smile on her face.

Sebastian could hardly sleep since he got that text that Serena was kissing another man. He couldn't believe it. For days he was waiting for her to tell him, but day by day she never told him anything. She was going to pay for this, no one makes a fool out of Sebastian. Sebastian called Cassie.

"Cassie, what is the update with Serena?"

"I am meeting her today. I will keep you posted my dear." Cassie said.

"Fine."

Cassie was waiting for Charlie when he came home.

"Aww, I care about you a lot? I heard you on the phone." He looked in the foyer and saw her siting in the chair.

"My god, you are completely whipped."

"Shut up."

"What happened to us?"

"Nothing has changed"

Yes it has. You love her, you don't love me anymore."

"It is just a game Cass." Cassie walked up to him and kissed him, but Charlie pushed her away.

"Look at you, and what you are reduced to, she has changed you. Wait, she doesn't know about your past does she? As her best friend it is my duty to tell her what you are up to." She got her phone out to call Serena.

"Put the phone down."

"Shh, this will only take a second." She whispered. Charlie took the phone away from her.

"I was thinking about telling her everything myself. I don't care what you say anymore."

"I forgot, you care for her. People don't change in one day. You and I are the same, we love games. Don't do it Charlie or you will end up a joke."

"I will take my chances." Cassie left as he said those words.

Serena went back to the apartment tired from her planing. She couldn't stop thinking about what happened with Charlie, she didn't know what to think anymore. She had to think about it and she had only one week to do it.

"You are home early." She turned and saw Sebastian sitting at the desk.

"Yeah, I needed a break from the wedding planning."

Sebastian went up to her and kissed her. "Good. How is it coming along?"

"It is good, it will be ready this week."

"I know what has been going on."

"What do you mean?" Sebastian wanted to say I know you kissed Charlie, but he didn't want anything ruining his wedding day. He was going to wait until after the wedding. After the wedding everything would change, for them. He was in control of everything and she would pay for what she did to him to make him into the fool.

"I saw the present you got me, sorry." She let out a breath, she wasn't ready to tell him anything until she really knew what she wanted.

"It is ok, you can wear the watch for the wedding."

"Thank you I really love it. You know I love a good watch." Serena kissed him on the cheek.

"I am really tired ok, I am going to go to take a nap before I meet Cassie." Serena went into the bedroom and laid down, she didn't know what to do, she was torn between if she should follow her heart or stick with what is easy. She was going to talk to Cassie later, but she really wanted to follow her heart.

Serena finally met up with Cassie at the Starbucks near Cassie's apartment.

"Hey Cass, it feels like forever since I have seen you."

"I know, I have been trying to get new clients, plus doing your wedding at the same time. I have been busy. What is it that you wanted to meet up about, you sounded sad." At that moment Serena's phone rang and she noticed it was Charlie.

"Hold on one second." She picked up her phone and got up and went inside Starbucks and into the bathroom to take the call.

"Hey Charlie, I am having lunch right now, can I call you back?"

"I will make this quick. I am messed up ok. I thought I cared about you, but it was just a lie. I just wanted to screw with your head and mess up your marriage. I don't care about you at all."

You don't mean that"

"You don't get it, I don't like you, you were just another conquest for me. Everything was just an act."

"You are messed up in the head! After the wedding I never want to see you again!" Serena hung up, and while she was crying she went back to the table.

"Sweetie what is wrong." Cassie said in a comforting tone.

"I cheated on Sebastian with Charlie. And I thought that there was a reason I met Charlie, whenever I saw him I felt a connection with him, more than I do with Sebastian, but he just called and said I was just a conquest. I can't believe I did this to Sebastian. I need to come clean."

"Oh sweetie, you shouldn't come clean, it is over, you already got your heart broken once, you shouldn't break it again. It is over between you and Charlie. Sebastian has no need to know."

"Thank you Cassie, I will just forget Charlie ever existed. I will marry Sebastian, he is the real love of my life anyway." Cassie hugged Serena while Cassie was smiling.

Sebastian's phone was ringing he answered it.

"Hello"

"Hey, Sebastian, its Cassie."

"What is the update Cass?"

"I am sorry but they did the deed. She even said that she was going to leave you for Charlie."

"She can't do that, I have done everything for her. No one leaves me and gets away with it."

"Well, at least you have me, you can leave her and come back to me."

"You don't get it, after I marry her I get her money and become rich since her father is rich. I am marrying her. I deserve that money. She is not going to do this to me now, when I am so close to the finish line."

"I know what I can do to help you with that, and you could also leave her. I will be in touch." Cassie hung up the phone angrily. She was not happy, Everyone wanted Serena. Serena was going to pay for this.

"What can I do for you" the person at the register said.

"I want to purchase a pistol please."

"Ok, that would be $110. Have a good day." Serena was going to rue the day she made a fool out of me. Her wedding day is something no one will ever forget. The person thought as they left the store.

Cassie got back to her apartment and went to drop her keys on her table. She turned and jumped. Finally noticing that Charlie was there.

"Shit, Charlie you scared me."

"Don't like people coming in unannounced do you? Now you know what it feels like."

"What are you doing here and what is with the champagne?"

"I thought you would like to know what happened between me and Serena. It is over."

"Really?"

"You were right I can't change. I thought we should celebrate. What do you want to toast to?"

"My triumph."

"Ok, whatever. To your triumph over Serena." Cassie laughed at that.

"What is so funny?"

"My dear Charlie, my triumph isn't over her, it is over you. You gave up on the first person you ever loved because

I threatened you. Don't you get it, You are still in love with her, but it made me smile to make you ashamed of that. You are just my toy I loved to play with and now I am done with you. Now you have officially blown it with her, I think it is the most pathetic thing I have ever seen and heard. Never get in a game that you can't win." Cassie smiled and took a sip of the champagne. "Haven't you heard, I am the bitch in this town, no one says they are done until I say so." Charlie stormed out of the apartment.

Serena saw that her phone was ringing, she noticed it was Charlie, and quickly ignored him. She didn't want to have anything to do with him anymore, especially the way he talked to her. She couldn't believe she almost broke off her wedding for a guy she only knew for a few weeks just because she thought they had a connection. She wasn't going to think about it anymore, she was done with him officially. After the wedding she never had to see him again.

Charlie went to Sebastian and Serena's house to try to explain what happened. He loved her he knew that much and she deserved the truth. He knocked on the door hoping Serena would answer, but Sebastian answered instead in nothing but a towel.

"Charlie, what a surprise, what do you want?"

"I need to talk to Serena is she here?"

"Oh, she is in the shower right now."

"Hey Sebastian I just took the last bit of the soap Serena uses, she needs more."

A woman called out from behind Sebastian. Charlie looked past Sebastian and saw Cassie standing in a towel. He couldn't believe it, Sebastian was cheating on Serena, she need to know.

"Wow Cassie, you wouldn't have done this if you didn't think I should know."

"This is a coincidence Charlie, I didn't expect to see you." Charlie faced Sebastian again.

"You need to tell Serena about this or I…"

"You will what, because Cassie has informed me that you have been having your own little trist with my girlfriend. You tell her anything you are done. No one is going to keep me away from my money that she has. Not even you. So turn around leave and forget you ever saw anything."

"What money?"

"Cass, I thought he knew about the money, that is why he was with her."

"Oops, did I say he knew, my mistake Sebastian."

"Forget everything or you will regret you even knew me or Serena." Sebastian slammed the door in Charlie's face, he was going to tell Serena the truth, it felt wrong lying to her. He would tell her everything one way or the other.

CHAPTER 8

One week later
The night before the wedding

"Tomorrow is the big day are you excited?" Cassie asked Serena as they did finishing touches on the boat.

"I am, I have waited for this day ever since I met Sebastian."

"Have you heard anything from Charlie?"

"No, not since he kept calling multiple times last week. He just stopped."

"Lets make a toast, to the wedding that no one will ever forget."

"Cheers to that."

"You better get some rest you are a wife starting tomorrow."

"And nothing will stop me from going down the aisle."
The Wedding Reception

Charlie didn't stop the wedding in time, Serena still married him even after he wrote her the letter. "I thought I would get the girl in the end" He said to himself. He would take the pictures she needed and leave her alone for good.

"Mrs. Smith…" Serena turned around and saw a waiter.

"I love hearing that. Is something wrong?"

"No, I have this package for you I wanted to give it to you before, but the wedding had already started. This person wanted you to open it immediately."

"Thank you, I appreciate it." Serena left to go below deck, the party was dying down and everyone was starting to get off the boat to go to the beach. She was able to sneak away. She got a champagne glass and went downstairs to the room where she and Sebastian were supposed to sneak off to, and closed the door behind her. She opened the package and found a note that could have been a book. She noticed that it was from Charlie.

"Serena, I don't know what to say to repair the damage that I have caused you. Being with you is the only time I have been happy and truly myself. My life has been a mystery and a joke, I loved playing games with other people, until, you. You were the person that wasn't a game, because I succeeded in hurting the first person I ever loved. Enclosing, I give you the truth, please read the other pages. No more lies, and no more hiding. Please give me another chance my dear Serena, I love you with all my heart and I mean that. Always and forever yours, Charlie." Serena put down the notes and read the other pages. "Oh my god." She said to herself surprised.

Serena was standing on the deck of a boat that had white lights on the rails and flower petals everywhere around her in her white wedding dress drinking champagne, she was looking out in the water, she turned around bringing the champagne glass down to her side and saw a gun pointed at her and had a sad worried look on her face.

"I never saw this coming any of it. Why did you betray me?" Serena said.

"Why, because you get whatever you want without any consequences, Sebastian, Charlie, you are just a whore who had to have both."

"Cass, how could you do this to me. You set me up from the beginning, you even toyed with Sebastian, and you have been having sex with him?"

Cassie laughed. "Oh Charlie, he got to you huh. I knew I should have dealt with him first. First you got the man I ever had feelings for and then when I moved on you had to get Charlie."

"I didn't know Charlie was yours, and we just happened. And you, you have been having sex with a man that doesn't even love me, he only wants my money. So you have him."

"No, I don't officially have him until you are out of the picture. We will get your money, I pretended to be your lawyer, I changed some things around for you. See if you die, Sebastian and I get your money you inherited from your father."

"All this so you could hurt me?"

"Exactly."

"I am so sorry."

"It is too late for apologies." Cassie pulled the trigger and shot Serena in the abdomen, when she didn't go down Cassie shot her again. Serena dropped the champagne glass that shattered when it hit the ground. Serena got pushed back and fell over the railing into the cold water it took only a few seconds and she closed her eyes. Cassie, put the gun in her purse while she smiled and walked away. With Everyone at the beach, and with all the music and festivities, no one will figure out that the bride is missing until that last possible moment.

"Sebastian, you look rather lonely." Sebastian turned around to see Cassie.

"Did you do it?"

"Yes I did, no one will find Serena, or figure out she is gone, it is like she never existed. And you are my alibi." Cassie went to kiss him on the lips.

"I am glad you told me what you did. Thank you for getting me that money, now that we both have it we can do anything we want."

"Of course we can. Now we can finally be together." Sebastian kissed Cassie passionately. Cassie and Sebastian stopped kissing when they heard Sirens. The sound was coming near the boat. They both ran as fast as they could, the boat was a walk away from the beach. They saw that people were gathered and the police were all over the boat searching and looking around.

"I thought you said no one would find her body Cassie!"

"Relax, she probably floated to the surface or something and someone saw her body. We just talk to the police, no one knows it was us who killed her." Cassie and Sebastian got through the crowd and went to talk to the police.

"Excuse me officer what is going on." Cassie said pretending to be surprised and concerned.

"Are you Cassie Blake? And are you the husband to Serena Bennet?

"Yes I am, and this is her husband, is something wrong? Did something happened to her?" Cassie said pretending to be worried.

"Cassie Blake, you are under arrest for the premeditated murder of Serena Bennet and Sebastian Smith you are under arrest as her accomplice for the planned murder of Serena."

"What!!!! This is absurd!!." As Sebastian said that and they were taking him away to the police car he saw Serena standing there with Charlie by her side.

"Cassie you said you had taken care of it, I can't believe I believed you." Cassie turned to see what Sebastian was talking about and she saw Serena.

"I killed you, it is not possible that you are here."

"Officer can my friend and I have a moment with these two before you take them away please. Oh and check her thoroughly when we are done, she didn't throw the gun in the ocean."

"Sure, just make it quick."

"I watched you die, I shot you and you fell in the water. How is it possible you are still alive?" Charlie handed Serena a glass of champagne.

"Cassie do you remember our toast? I would like to make a toast now, to my triumph."

"What the hell are you talking about?"

"Would you like to do the honors Charlie?"

"No, you are the one who got shot, you should be the one to tell them Serena."

CHAPTER 9

Few hours earlier

"Oh my god." Serena said with surprise. She left the room and rushed to find Charlie. "Where is everyone" she said to herself. She looked around the deck and no one was on the boat. She went off the boat and ran until she got to the beach. She finally spotted Charlie at the bar.

"Charlie!!" She screamed. Charlie turned around and ran toward her. When she stopped he noticed that she was out of breath.

"Are you ok, what is wrong?"

"Can we go back to the boat for a second?"

"Yeah sure." He motioned to someone that he was leaving.

"Oh, I am sorry, you are with someone."

"Oh no, I am not, it is fine, I can go with you." They both walked back to the boat, while Serena was unaware that they were being followed. When they finally got back to the boat, Serena took him to the room.

"Is this the truth?"

"Is what the truth Serena?"

"Everything you wrote in this letter. Or is this some more of your lies."

"Like I said in the letter, no more lies, no more mystery. This is me. I hope that you can forgive me, and I hope you give me a second chance. I…I love you too much to hurt you or to watch other people hurt you." Charlie walked up to Serena and was inches away from her. "You are the only person who knows the real me and I will do anything to get you to forgive me, even if it takes a lifetime. I am going to count to three and then I am going to pick you up and put you on that bed and kiss you. If you don't want me to, walk out that door right now. One….two….." He didn't finish Serena kissed him passionately on the lips. Charlie picked her up and laid her on the bed and he continued kissing her. Serena put her hands on his chest to stop the kiss.

"What is it Serena?"

"Even after everything you told me, I am still married." Charlie smiled.

"No you are not. Charlie stood up and took Serena's hands to help her up. "You three can come in now." Three people walked in, but she didn't recognize them.

"Serena, meet my friends Ashley, Samantha, and Hunter."

"That is the minister."

"Yeah, I wouldn't call myself a minister, I actually just help him get his pictures and art work sold. Hunter said smiling.

"Charlie what is…"

"I knew that Sebastian just wanted your father's money. Ashley and Sam here are police officers, so I asked if they could keep an eye on Sebastian and Cassie for me while I looked out for you. They found out that Cassie, changed things around so Sebastian can get your money and she could get your money. Samantha went in and told the lawyer what had happened and he changed it back so you can still get the money and you alone. And I would tell you the truth no matter what, so for one thing you are not really married." Charlie said with an awkward smile.

"How is that possible?"

"Well Charlie told me what was going on with you and told me all about it, so I offered to help. I played a minister for you and you signed fake papers for a marriage license. The party was really fun though, I got a girls number which was awesome."

"Hunter really." Ashley said. "In other words we got you out of a really bad predicament."

"Why would you all do this for me?"

"Well, Charlie did it because he loves you duh, even if he was a mean, arrogant, ass…"

"Sam, point." Charlie said

"Sorry, oh, he does love you and you are the first person to make him happy. The three of us did it because Charlie is like family to us, he gets hurt we hurt someone for hurting him. And since he is family and he loves you, you are like part of the family too or whatever. Sam said smiling.

"There is one more thing I need to tell you, they are planning on killing you tonight because they both want the money and they want to run away together."

"What!!!"

"We are going to arrest them before they can do anything." Ashley said reassuringly.

"No."

"No? Look girly, they are going to kill you if we don't arrest them now." Hunter said

"Look, I want to know why Cassie is doing this ok. She owes me that much."

"If you get shot…"

"She won't. Take off your dress." Sam said.

"Sorry sweetie, you seem like a great girl, but your not really my type." Serena said smiling. Sam threw her blouse at Serena.

"Pushing it. This is a bullet proof corset made for me, I know a person. Anyway I wore it tonight just in case. Ashley and I will tell the other officers to stand down, and then after she shoots you, well if she does we will wait a while then get them and arrest them. I can understand why you would want closure."

"Thank you Sam."

Serena dropped the champagne glass that shattered when it hit the ground. Serena got pushed back and fell over the railing into the cold water it took only a few seconds and she closed her eyes. Serena sunk down in the water and opened her eyes, and quickly held her breath. She waited a few minutes to give time for Cassie to leave. After fourteen minutes Serena swam back up to the surface and gasped for air. She swam to shore where Charlie and Hunter were waiting for her.

"Shit!! Getting shot really hurts." Serena said angrily Charlie helped her out of the water and put a blanket around her.

"So closure, did you get any?" Hunter said smiling.

"I will hit you. But yes I did, you can call Ashley and Sam they can arrest them now." Hunter laughed and walked away to make a call.

"Are you ok?" Charlie asked Serena now that they were alone.

"I am just peachy keen. Thank you Charlie for everything. You didn't have to do this."

"I did, I am the one that hurt you, I owed you one."

"Is that the only reason?"

"No, I love you that is the other reason, I knew we had a connection when we first met. I love you Serena Bennet. What do you say to that?"

"I love you too Charlie, and you have already paid your debt, the only thing I ask of you is to love me unconditionally forever."

"I will have no trouble doing that my dear." Charlie picked her up in his arms and kissed her.

Presently...

"You counted me out before we even finished our little game Cassie. Don't start a game you can't win, isn't that what you said?"

"Screw you. Charlie."

"Never fuck with the king of games, you will loose every time." Serena walked to Cassie and Sebastian.

"There there, Cassie and Sebastian, at least you two still have each other in jail." Serena said smiling. "We are done now you can take them away."

"This isn't over Serena I will be back." Sebastian said angrily.

"Aww sweetie, it is ok, I think you will meet a lot of guys who want you. I can move on." Serena said while laughing.

"What do you want to do now my dear?"

"Well Charlie let's go home, well your home, and then we can kiss, and spend the rest of our lives together."

"Sounds like a plan. I finally got the girl of my dreams." Charlie said smiling. Serena kissed him on the lips. She finally found true happiness, and found someone who truly loves her.

TRUTH OR LIE

PROLOGUE

"Behind door number one is…" Cassie looked at the stranger who had been giving her hell all day. She didn't even know how she got here or why these people were doing this to her. Why were these strangers after her and her family, she just couldn't understand it. I wish I could see who these people were, she thought angrily to herself. They were all wearing masks. Their voices sounded familiar, but she couldn't put her finger on their voices alone. When the door opened she couldn't believe who was behind the door. His hands were tied behind his back, with tape over his mouth. There was a gash on his forward where he was hit with something. Two people had brought him out and put him in front of her and put him on his knees. When he looked up at Cassie, he screamed out hysterically. The person holding one of his shoulders hit him on his head to make him be quiet.

"What is the meaning of this? What the hell is going on, where is my family??!!" Cassie yelled.

"This is the last stop of our game my dear. This will prove what your family is worth to you." The man stated calmly. The man handed her a gun.

"Before you think to take the shot don't bother, I have another gun and there is another person in hiding just waiting for something to happen so he can take the shot. Now, Let us put your love to the test shall we. I want you to shoot this man, if you do that then your family will be returned to you and this will all be but just a dream."

"Why him, I can't just shoot him."

"Why? Do you know him?"

"No, I don't, but I just can't kill someone." Cassie whispered.

"All part of the game my dear. Are you going to save a stranger you barely know, or your family, the clock is ticking." The man stated. Cassie couldn't believe this, she couldn't shoot him, she loved him too much to do just that. She was looking down at the gun, not knowing what to do. She looked back up and looked at the man in the eyes, she pointed the gun at him. The man's eyes went big with fear.

"Time is up what are you going to do?"

CHAPTER 1

A couple hours earlier
8:00 AM

Cassie turned on her side in bed, she opened her eyes slowly to a surprise. She sat up in bed and took the rose in her hands and then put it down on the nightstand and took the note that read open me. "Come down stairs and there will be a surprise for you when you come down. Love Vince." When Cassie finished reading the letter she went to get ready for her big surprise.

Vince was almost done preparing breakfast for Cassie, today was their anniversary so he wanted everything to be perfect before he went off to work. He couldn't believe they had been married for four years now starting tomorrow. When he turned around after finishing the pancakes, he saw Cassie sitting at the kitchen table. She was so beautiful he thought, with her long brown hair, brown eyes. She always had a beautiful smile on her face. She was wearing her leather jacket, a dark blue crop top, blue jeans, and black boots. He went over and put the pancakes and the glass of orange juice right in front of her and kissed her on the lips.

"Happy anniversary my sweet Cassie."

"You too sweetie. But it is not until tomorrow. I can't believe you did this." Cassie smiled as she took her first bite of the pancakes.

"Call it a pre anniversary. I have another present for you, I have another book coming out soon. I wanted you to be the first one to read it. It will be on the shelves by next week." Vince said smiling.

"I didn't know you were writing another book, what is this one about?"

"That is a surprise." Vince went to the living room to pull the book out of the bag and went back to the kitchen table and placed the book right in front of her. "I thought since you were the quickest person I know that could read a book, I figured you could finish it in a couple of hours, especially since it is not that long."

"Of course honey, The Lying Game. I am definitely intrigued. I will let you know what I think of it later tonight."

"You should turn to the page after the title page." Vince said anxiously.

"Ok. When she turned to that page she noticed a dedication page and the whole story was dedicated to her. She looked up and smiled. He bent down to kiss her on the lips. She put the book down and put her hands on his chest. "Don't you have to go into work?"

"Well, I was thinking of staying home today you know, so we can spend the whole day together for our anniversary. Those are the perks of being editor of a publishing company."

"I thought you had that meeting with Holly."

"Holly understands it is a special day today, she even encouraged me to take the day off, since I have been working long hours lately."

"What about the meeting with that writer, don't you need to talk to him about the finishing touches of his story, and plus I thought you were going to hang out with him today."

"If I didn't know any better I would think you were trying to get rid of me." Vince said standing back up with his arms crossed.

"I just think you shouldn't take off work just for me, plus Rebecca is coming over today."

"What are you planning with your sister huh?"

"It is a surprise for you of course. You won't know until tonight. I can't work on the surprise if you are in the house all day." Cassie said smiling sweetly hoping he wouldn't notice that she was lying.

"Ok honey, I am looking forward to the surprise. I will call Holly and tell her I am coming in. I will cook dinner tonight my dear. I am going to go head up and dress."

"Ok." That was close Cassie thought, she didn't want her husband to find out the real truth of why she was kicking him out so early. When he came back downstairs she had to admit he was sexy, and very sweet a good combination of why she fell in love with him in the first place. He had short dark brown hair, and brown eyes. He was wearing his red and black plaid shirt with the sleeves rolled up, dark blue jeans and brown boots. Her sexy writer ready to finally get out the door.

"So, I will be back tonight to cook us a romantic dinner and we can stay in and watch a movie, I have a great surprise for you tonight, I am hoping this will be one anniversary that you will never forget." Vince kissed her on the cheek. And as she saw him ride off on his motorcycle she went upstairs to put on some make up to get ready for the real man in her life who she truly loved. She couldn't wait to see Tyler. Tyler was sexy, muscular, smart funny, so cool. He was her bad boy. He was very sexy with his with dark black hair and icy blue eyes. He looked both dangerous even in his sexy sweaters, blue jeans, and black shoes that he always wore. He was truly a gentleman with a little danger. He also had five silver earrings. Three on his left ear cartilage and two on his right bottom. Oddly enough she didn't really feel bad about what she was doing to Vince. Soon she would be leaving with most of his money in hand and being with him will be but a memory What Vince didn't know is that she and Tyler had been stealing money from him for two years now. Soon with the separate account she had she would have enough stashed away so she could leave Vince for good. She went downstairs to wait for her beau, yes she was the only person who would call him that and soon Tyler would be her one and only. She sat down and read the new book that Vince had written, just to past the time until her man arrived.

CHAPTER 2

3:00 pm

Cassie woke up a couple of hours later, she checked her watch and noticed it was already a little past three in the afternoon, she wondered where Tyler was, he would have been here by now. She tried calling him on his cell phone, but it had went straight to voicemail. She was a little surprised her sister hadn't come yet as well, or at least called her by now. Cassie tried to call her sister, but it also went straight to voicemail. She left her sister a message and went to go upstairs to get her purse to get ready to go to the cafe to meet her sister instead of meeting her at her house. As she was walking she felt something on her shoe as she walked. She looked down and noticed a trail of gummy bears, her favorite candy as a kid. She looked around looking for someone to pop up at anytime. She decided to follow the trail skeptically, she stopped at the stairs when she saw a note on the steps. "Enjoy the sweets, let the game begin. Love Ty." She let out a gentle breath realizing that this was all Tyler's doing. He must have snuck in here to do this, he is very sweet she thought. She went up the stairs and followed the rest of the trail of gummy bears, she stopped when the trail led her to the king sized bed, she saw an iPad sitting in the middle of a heart shaped design of gummy bears. She saw another note that read play me. What she saw on the video made her go weak in the knees. She slowly sat down on the bed with one hand covering her mouth and the other hand weakly on the iPad. She was looking at her sister, but she wasn't her usual care free goofy self. She was scared, she could see it in her brown eyes as she noticed she was holding back tears, and her long brown hair was tousled, her hands were tied behind her back and her blue dress was unkempt. Who would do this to her sister she thought.

"Say what I told you. What do you have to say to your dear sweet sister?" Cassie heard a strange man say, she couldn't see the man's face, but his voice sounded oddly familiar, but she couldn't place it at all, she didn't know anyone who would do this to her family.

"Cass...Cassie," Her sister said between sobs." I have been kidnapped, and you are not allowed to call the police or anyone you know, you have to play the game and follow their instructions in order to get your family back, if you don't then you will be killing your family and they will find your friends one by one until you have nothing left. Please, help me." The video cut off there. She couldn't believe this was happening, she dropped the iPad on the floor as she stood up to get to the phone quickly she needed to call someone, the police, Vince, or Tyler. Just to make sure they were ok, and nothing happened to them. When she picked up the phone she didn't hear a dial tone.

"Your phone line is dead, you just got one rule and you are already trying to break it, this is going to be fun. I love when they try to break rules." Cassie turned around quickly at the strangers voice. He had a bored attitude while standing in the entryway to the bedroom. He had a muscular build, he had short brown hair, and brown eyes, His white shirt was unbuttoned and he was wearing black jeans with black and white converse. He had a tattoo in the shape of a flame on his right arm. He had a gun pointed right at her He had a mask on so she couldn't really tell who he was.

"What the hell do you want, why are you doing this?"

"You will see soon enough, right now, the games shall begin. I am going to ask you two questions right now, it is up to you to tell the truth or not, if I know you are lying then we are going on a little trip. Sounds fun right?"

"Go to hell, I am not playing your stupid sick game."

"I don't think you really have a choice in the matter, unless you want to let your sister die now." The man went for his phone, but Cassie put up her hand.

"Wait, fine, just please don't hurt her."

"I will make the first two easy for you. First question, where do you work?"

"I work as a film critic for New York Magazine. What is the other?"

"My second question, I see that you and your husband Vince, have a joint account, is there any more than what you have in that account?"

"No, there isn't, that is all we have." Cassie answered, this person doesn't know them she thought, so he wouldn't know about her other account.

"It is time to go for a ride. Join me won't you." The stranger said.

"Why I answered your questions."

"With questions, come the obstacles to get your loved ones back. Lets go. You are driving."

CHAPTER 3

4:00 pm

When he finally told her to stop they were sitting at the bank that she and Vince have gone to, to create their accounts.

"What are we doing here?"

"I want you to take all the money out of this account and put it in another one, come back in the car and we will continue this game." He handed Cassie a piece of paper, and she noticed right away that it was the separate account that she had created.

"Why do you want money out of this particular account?"

"It doesn't matter why, all that matters is that you transfer all the money. I will know if you don't. If you try anything I will know, someone I know will be watching your every move. You can go now."

Cassie strides to the information desk when she entered the bank.

"May I help you ma'am?" The young woman asked with a bright smile on her face.

"I would like to withdraw a large sum of money from an account and transfer it into another one."

"This way ma'am." The young lady leads her to a small office and gestures for Cassie to sit in a chair in front of a desk with a computer and a phone. "How much will you be transferring to this account?"

"All of the eighty-thousand dollars."

"May I see some ID please?" Cassie showed her ID and the account numbers. "Wait here for a second please. When the woman came back she handed Cassie the phone. "Tyler Gilbert is on the phone for you ma'am." Cassie took the phone and let out sigh. She couldn't let Tyler know what was going on. Or she could try since no one else was in here, he could get help. "Could you give me some privacy please?"

"Of course ma'am." After she left the room, Cassie put the phone to her ear.

"Tyler, thank god, are you ok?"

"Yeah I am fine, what is going on, this lady told me you were pulling all the money out of the account, what is wrong."

"I have no idea. These guys have kidnapped my sister and I don't know what the hell is happening and they want me to transfer all the money out the account, I am so freaked the hell out Tyler I don't know what to do."

"Calm down sweetie, what can I do? You can transfer the money, you should."

"Can you call the police, I mean they said I shouldn't, but I will just feel safer if you would, please."

"Yes, just make sure you do what they say." The woman came back into the room. "Hand the phone back so I can tell her it is ok to transfer the money. It will be ok Cass."

"Thanks Ty." Cassie handed the phone back to the young woman. After she got off the phone she transferred the money into the other account. Cassie was hoping that Tyler was calling the cops and could find her sister before something bad happened to her. She just hoped that she could keep these guys busy while he did it. She got back into the car and into the driver's seat.

"It is done. I transferred the money, I have the proof if you want to see it." Cassie said angrily.

"So angry, calm down a bit. I believe you. Now we are going somewhere else. I want you to drive to the publishing company that your husband works."

"Why?"

"You have no room for asking questions, that is not part of the game. Just drive before you kill your sister."

"Fine." Cassie started driving to where her husband worked.

CHAPTER 4

7:00 pm

"Stop right here." The man said as they parked a few blocks away from the Undercover Between the Lines Publishing company where Vince worked.

"Why are we parked right here? And why did you want me to come here."

"All in good time. Just sit back and watch the show my dear." As she saw Vince walking out of the building, she wished she could tell him what was going on send him some kind of warning. She didn't want him to get hurt as well. All of a sudden a black van came by and two people jumped out and took hold of Vince she watched how he struggled to get away, but one of them punched him in the face to knock him out, and pushed him into the van. She heard something high pitched, it sounding like an alarm going off, but she finally realized it was her screams. She turned right around to face the man responsible for all of this.

"Why??!!!" She screamed hitting the man. He pointed the gun at her and that made her sit still and stop screaming.

"You broke a rule. You shouldn't have tried to call the police, but don't worry you will have a chance to get your husband back and your sister. As long as you follow the rules and you don't break them again." Cassie was too stunned to talk, how did he know she told Tyler to call the police she thought. Now Vince was kidnapped as well and it is all her fault that the man she loved was kidnapped and his life along with her sister's were hanging in the balance.

"Fine, I won't disobey again."

"Good. Now you get one question at the moment. It is a hypothetical. If there was a chance for you in your company to move ahead, and bump up from just being a film critic would you do anything to get there even steal another person's work?"

"No, I would provide my boss articles so he can see that I am a hard worker. I like to prove myself."

"Ok. We are going to take a drive somewhere. Start driving and I will lead you there." Cassie wondered where they could be going next, she just had to make sure to do anything he said to get her loved ones back.

CHAPTER 5

9:00 pm

When the man told her to stop they were right in front of the New York Magazine building. The man turned to face her and handed her two envelopes.

"Now, you have a choice on which envelope to hand your boss. You are not allowed to look in them. Just know that they are both articles that we want to go in the magazine. If you look in the envelopes I will know, just know that one can either destroy your career or lead you to great things. Look at the titles carefully. One is the Number One Lesson and the other is Undercover. Now you can go."

She walked into the building. Destroy my career, she thought, they must have figured out I forge everything and take everything from Rebecca. She didn't know what to do, she couldn't look into the envelopes because she knew something would happen. She waited at the front desk for her boss Smith, She had to figure it out before he came. Undercover is too obvious I take Rebecca's work when she is not looking so I do it like I am undercover she thought. But the Number One Lesson, it may be to not steal other's people work to get ahead she thought. She looked up and noticed Smith walking over to her, to her he was moving so slowly, like time was slowing down, this could kill her career as a critic for good and get her fired. The time had finally arrived her heart was beating quickly as Smith had finally reached her.

"Cassie, what is it? I got a call saying that you had an article for me?"

"Yeah, this one." She passed him the Undercover envelope. "I am sorry Smith, I have to go." She walked away quickly so she wouldn't know what it was, she would know soon enough, she just wanted to hurry to get her loved ones back. When she got in the car the man was waiting for her in the passenger seat. She handed him the other envelope.

"I see you gave him the Undercover one, interesting. So one last stop to make. It will take a couple of hours, I have already gassed the car up, I will guide you to this last place. Be happy, we are at the home stretch of you getting your loved ones back."

CHAPTER 6

11:12 pm

They finally arrived at a cabin, there was no other neighbor for miles.

"Go ahead and get out." Cassie got out of the car and the man came around and led her to the entryway to the cabin. They walked in and the cabin felt familiar like she had been there before. Seeing the white couch and the fire place in front of the couch, with the fluffy white soft carpet underneath her feet. Even the small kitchen to her right seemed very familiar. The man made her sit on the couch and told her to wait there. When he came back he stood in front of her.

"Now we have come to the end of the road, for you to choose. Here comes the very last question and obstacle to get your loved ones back. To see if you truly care to want them back."

"What is the hell is the question so we can end this already?"

"You are very eager, that is good. Lets play what is behind that door." He pointed to a room that was close to the kitchen, she could have sworn she had been here before.

She couldn't know what was behind that door, she hoped it was her sister and Vince.

"Behind door number one is…" Cassie looked at the stranger who had been giving her hell all day. She didn't even know how she got here or why these people were doing this to her. Why were these strangers after her and her family, she just couldn't understand it? I wish I could see who these people were, she thought angrily to herself. They were all wearing masks. Their voices sounded familiar, but she couldn't put her finger on their voices alone. When the door opened she couldn't believe who was behind the door. His hands were tied behind his back, with tape over his mouth. There was a gash on his forward where he was hit with something. Tyler she thought, that is how they knew that she had called the police, they had already had Tyler, and they heard the whole conversation. Now they had three people that she cared most about. Two people had brought him out and put him in front of her and put him on his knees. When he looked up at Cassie, he screamed out hysterically. The person holding one of his shoulders Hit him on his head to make him be quiet.

"What is the meaning of this? What the hell is going on, where is my family??!!" Cassie yelled.

"This is the last stop of our game my dear. This will prove what your family is worth to you." The man stated calmly. The man handed her a gun.

"Before you think to take the shot don't bother, I have another gun and there is another person in hiding just waiting for something to happen so he can take the shot. Now, Let us put your love to the test shall we, I want you to shoot this man, if you do that then your family will be returned to you and this will all be but just a dream."

"Why him, I can't just shoot him."

"Why. Do you know him? Is he special to you?" Yes, he is Cassie thought, but he couldn't know how special he was to her, otherwise Vince would know the truth and she couldn't have that. Cassie stood up slowly making sure that she didn't show anything towards Tyler to give away that she loved him.

"No, I don't, but I just can't kill someone." Cassie whispered.

"All part of the game my dear. Are you going to save a stranger you barely know, or your family, which means more to you? Who are you willing to loose to save the other, the clock is ticking." The man stated. Cassie couldn't believe this, she couldn't shoot him, she loved him too much to do just that. She was looking down at the gun, not knowing what to do. She looked back up and looked at the man in the eyes, she pointed the gun at him. The man's eyes went big.

"Time is up what are you going to do?" Cassie's hand was shaking she couldn't pull the trigger, she just couldn't. She lowered the gun slowly and was crying. She lowered to her knees right in front of Tyler. She put her head in her hands and started crying. "I can't, I just can't." She said muffled in her hands.

"I see, and why is it that you can't seem to kill this one person, especially knowing that it would save your family?" The man wasn't the one to speak this time, it was a woman, her voice sounded familiar but she wasn't truly paying attention, it was time she said it out loud even if it was to kidnappers.

"I care about him, I love him." Cassie said while tears were streaming down her face.

"More than your husband or your sister?"

"Yes, I have for a while." All of a sudden a clap came from the stairs. Cassie looked up startled, she saw the one person that she never thought she would see behind this.

CHAPTER 7

Four months ago

Vince was getting dressed and ready to go to work. Cassie had been more distant than ever before. He was going to try to come home early to talk about it more. When he went to the closet to get dressed he accidentally stepped on a big box. He looked down and saw it was a present. Maybe that is why she was acting so distant he thought, she was getting him a gift. No harm than for him to take a peek. When he looked inside he saw lingerie, two wine glasses, and a bottle of wine. He noticed there was a card and a teddy bear. "Happy anniversary to the best man in the world, something special is definitely in store for you tonight. To Tyler from your secret admirer." Tyler Vince thought, who the hell is Tyler? She is cheating on me, if so for how long and was it under his own roof? He couldn't believe she would do this. He didn't know what to say.

"Vince?" Vince quickly closed the box and put it back where it was and got his plaid shirt out and put it on.

"In here Cass, I just needed a shirt."

"So are you coming home late again?"

"Yeah I am, I won't be home until ten tonight. What will you be doing?"

"Oh nothing, probably just relaxing, Rebecca and I will be having a girls night." Liar he thought in his head.

"Ok, I will see you tonight then." Vince kissed her on the forehead and headed into the office.

While Vince finished up his book he heard a knock on the door.

"Come in."

"Hey, Vince, I need you to check out a few things and also Charlie is here to talk about his book with you."

"Holly, I finally finished my book."

"You did, congratulations, can I read it?"

"Of course I sent it to you, I have been working on it all morning. I had to rewrite everything and took a whole different turn to it. I got strangely and oddly inspired today."

"Are you ok, you seem a little frantic. I am your friend you can tell me anything you know."

"I know Holls, don't worry about it, I will tell you soon enough. Please just let me know what you think about my story huh."

"Sure, I am here if you need me." Holly closed the door. Vince had to calm himself down. Maybe there was an explanation for this. He needed help, he couldn't just do this on his own. He called the one people who he trusted the most.

"Hello, Becca, it is Vince I need you to do me a favor that you are going to find weird, I will have my friend Charlie fill you in when he meets you."

CHAPTER 8

A few weeks later

Holly went to see Vince after she finally read the book, she went to Bubba Gumps to meet him there for lunch. When she got there she stopped as she saw Vince, but he wasn't alone, he was with Charlie and another woman.

"Holly you are here, now the meeting can begin."

"Vince, I thought we were going to discuss your book." Holly stated.

"We are, what did you think?"

"It was nothing you have ever written before, I could feel your anger as you wrote this, and you wrote this in one day, what is going on."

"Well, Cassie has been cheating on me, that is where I got the inspiration from."

"Vince I am so sorry, have you confronted her?"

"Not yet, I have been talking to lawyers and I had Charlie and Rebecca here my sister in law to follow her for me while I kept close tabs on her at home."

"Ok, don't you think you should just let it sink in and divorce her."

"I thought about that until what they found and what I found. Charlie, what did you find?"

"Cassie and Tyler have been stealing money. Vince found this first as he noticed some money was missing from their joint account. When we followed her she had been stealing money from that account and transferring it to another account in her name that Tyler had access to."

"She hadn't just been stealing money from him, but from me as well, my own sister, not only that I found out she has been copying my work and passing it off as her own." Rebecca said angrily.

"That is horrible, what did your lawyer say." Holly asked.

"Knowing the things we do and having proof, she won't get anything of mine. I already have an apartment I want to move into, I am selling the house. Throughout everything I just want to make her pay. She has been lying to us for too long. I gave her everything and she destroyed it. Even was mean to her own sister." Holly put her hand on Vince's shoulder.

"I am truly sorry Vince, you too Rebecca. No one should do this to the ones they love."

"Your book."

"My book, what about it Charlie?"

"When you were writing it, were you thinking about Cassie?"

"I was actually."

"We could do the same thing that the characters do in your book, we just have to plan it."

"I don't know Charlie, that book was kind of harsh, and someone could get hurt." Holly said concerned.

"No, think about it, we wouldn't really hurt anyone, just get her to tell the truth, we fake kidnapping Rebecca, fake kidnapping Vince, but we kidnap Tyler, but not hurt him. Make her feel what you felt. To feel how hard it is to lose everything for once. It is the perfect revenge. She has lied to you both, you two deserve the truth." Rebecca and Vince looked at each other skeptical.

"I have always wanted to dabble in acting. I say we do it. She deserves it." Rebecca stated.

"I am in, it could actually be fun, especially to see the look on her face, when she finds out you are behind the whole thing Vince. Whatever you want to do we are behind you, if you don't want to we won't. But it is your call." Holly said reassuringly. Vince thought about it for a minute, maybe it was too harsh, but she has done so many wrong things too many times.

"Lets get planning." Vince said smiling.

Present: Midnight.

All of a sudden a clap came from the stairs. Cassie looked up startled, she saw the one person that she never thought she would see behind this.

"Vince, you are ok, what the hell is going on here?"

"It is midnight, my sweet wife, Happy anniversary, I told you it would be one that you would never forget. Did you enjoy my book?" Vince was walking towards her smiling a devilish smile.

"You did this, why would you do that? Your book? Why...?" Cassie whispered looking up into his eyes. Cassie thought for a second, she remembered where she knows this cabin from, from his book. This whole thing followed his book. "The book you dedicated to me, the book followed everything you did. Why?"

"Why, my dear." Vince sat down on his legs and tried to touch Cassie's cheek with his hand, but Cassie moved her head away. Vince chuckled and closed his hand and put it back to his side and stood back up. "I have known for a while what you were doing. Where you were, whose money you were stealing. I first found out when I found that present for Tyler here four months ago. The one with the lingerie and the wine. Thinking it was a gift for me. I had you followed. I planned this. You can remove your masks now." When they all removed their masks, Cassie was shocked, they all had smiles on their face, she saw Holly standing there, and the person she was surprised to see was her sister. Cassie stood up slowly to face her sister.

"Why would you do this Rebecca, my own sister? Why would you betray me like this?"

"Talk about betraying, Cass, stealing money from me and Vince. Cheating on him wasn't enough for you, you had to steal money too, and wait, on top of that since Charlie was keeping a close watch on you and Vince, I had to find out from them that my own sister was stealing my stories and passing them on as her own. Oh, wrong envelope by the way, you just told the boss that you were turning in my stories. He called me to see what was going on and I told him the truth and sent him proof that all the stories you turned in were really mine." Rebecca said. Cassie had a stunned look on her face she didn't know what to say, she had lost everything in that moment. She was on the verge of tears. She ran up to Vince.

"Vince this is not true, Tyler forced me to do all of it, you have to understand, he did all this to make me look like the bad guy. I have always loved you and only you. You know that." Cassie stated frantically looking into Vince's eyes. Vince put his hand softly on her cheek.

"Oh my dear Cass, now you know what it feels like to lose everything. I sold the house, we have a couple of weeks to get our things out, and I have already talked to my lawyer, you will not be getting anything of mine. That account your money went into was an account for me and your sister to get our money back. You and Tyler are free to go. The gash on his head is just effect. He is fine, we didn't touch him, just scared him. The blood isn't real it is makeup. The guns were never loaded, they were toys. After tonight, I am done with you, I hope you fix your ways unless you will be alone for the rest of your life. The only person you will have by your side is Tyler. Good bye Cass. And oh, in the other envelope are divorce papers, I have already signed them. It is your turn. If you come after any of us, we have proof of everything you did, we could send you to jail if we wanted to." Vince, Holly, Charlie, and Rebecca all turned their backs to her and walked out of the cabin. Cassie untied Tyler and they both left the cabin.

One year later

Vince and Charlie were at their book signing for both of their books since they came out at the same time.

"Looks like I have a longer line than you huh?" Charlie said smiling.

"Oh we shall see. Loser buying drinks?"

"Of course."

"Now, now boys, why does it have to be a competition. Besides we all know my fiancé will win of course." Holly said while walking towards Vince.

"Of course you would side with Vince, but you are bet commissioner, you are not allowed to take sides." Charlie stated while laughing.

"Oh, she can take my side anytime." Vince kissed Holly on the lips.

"Get a room you two." Rebecca said walking up to the tables.

"Rebecca, I see that you stopped by, to get your copy of my book signed right." Charlie said winking.

"Oh yeah, Holly did say you two had a bet going on. How about this, I have both of your books and you both will be even, one to one." Rebecca laughed

"Party pooper. Oh looks like they are starting to let people in, let the game begin Charlie." Vince was finally happy with all of his friends and family with him, and he finally found the love of his life who he could trust now and forever.

Printed in the United States
By Bookmasters